A WOMAN'S OWN MYSTERY

Also by Hannah Wakefield
The Price You Pay

A Woman's Own Mystery

St. Martin's Press
New York

A WOMAN'S OWN MYSTERY. Copyright © 1990 by Hannah Wakefield. All rights reserved. Printed in the United States of America. No part of this book may be used or reproduced in any manner whatsoever without written permission except in the case of brief quotations embodied in critical articles or reviews. For information, address St. Martin's Press, 175 Fifth Avenue, New York, N.Y. 10010.

Library of Congress Cataloging-in-Publication Data
Wakefield, Hannah.
   A woman's own mystery / Hannah Wakefield.
     p.   cm.
   ISBN 0-312-05539-0
   I. Title.
PR6073.A3738W66   1991
823'.914—dc20   90-15553
                                                                         CIP

First published in Great Britain by The Women's Press Limited under the title *A February Mourning*.

First U.S. Edition: March 1991
10 9 8 7 6 5 4 3 2 1

One

Am I dead? This is my first thought as I come to.

I am lying on my back in pitch blackness and my mind seems to be a long way off, swaddled in gauze and cotton wool. I want to rub my eyes but can't lift my hand. I can't lift my head either, or my foot.

What's the name of that disease the Victorians feared so much – the one where you're taken for dead but you're really alive in there, you just can't communicate?

Narcolepsy?

Catalepsy?

Do I have it? Is this why it's so dark – because I'm in a coffin?

Too benumbed even to panic I begin to investigate outwards along the inside of my skin and this way locate pockets of sweat drying under my arms and between my breasts, which are tender. Covering me from the top of my head down to my ankles is a heavy rug which smells faintly of paint thinner and something else, something rotten. I run my tongue around my lips and the taste connects to the smell: dried sick.

Awful.

I go back to my fingers and this time when I try to wiggle them, succeed. The energy spreads to the whole of my right hand, which I manage to move (or think I'm moving) a couple of inches. If this is a coffin it's a roomy one with a lumpy foam mattress.

Sound impinges – a rushing with soft regular thumpings which at first I take for the coursing of my blood and the working of my heart. Then I become aware of movement and decide the sound is outside me: tyres on a wet road. I'm in a car, I must be in a car.

Yes – there: feel the gentle braking – the idling – the slow acceleration.

Am I in the trunk? No, that's impossible. I'm stretched out to my full length. I can even move my toes now and lift my head.

Why can't I remember where I am or how I got here?

Am I concussed? Drugged? Seriously ill?

The panic inconceivable a moment earlier begins to stir and to calm myself I close my eyes and stare into the blackness behind my eyelids. As I wait and watch, a memory gradually begins to emerge around this very sickliness I'm so eager to shake. This isn't the first time I've been ill recently. I was ill – when was it now? Just the other day.

I

You get a feeling when a client's going to pull a no-show in court and I woke up that Friday morning with that feeling about Gillian Shiraz. It had been two days since she'd phoned me to say her friend and character witness had disappeared to tend to some unknown personal matter thirty-six hours earlier and hadn't been seen since. She'd been trying to sound cool but Gillian's not a cool woman: anxiety, on the march from her solar plexus, was on the point of capturing her entire chest cavity. 'I can't face him alone,' she'd said. 'I just can't.' 'Him' was her ex-husband, Tonio, who was challenging her custody of their daughter.

I'd taken down the number of the public phone box she was calling from, rung her back, and kept another client waiting twenty minutes while I'd attempted to soothe her. I thought I'd almost succeeded too but she'd been supposed to check in with me by six o'clock the previous evening and there'd been not a word.

The feeling became increasingly oppressive as I dressed, so much so that the mere thought of breakfast made me slightly nauseated, and by the time I reached the bathroom I actively wanted to be sick to my stomach. I knelt on the bathroom rug beside the toilet bowl waiting (hoping) but nothing happened and after two or three minutes the feeling gradually subsided into slight nausea once more. I got to my feet again, pulled the light switch on and, as I looked into my own startled eyes staring back at me from the mirror, found myself face to face with a certain awkward little truth I'd been attempting not to see: my period was overdue.

I counted back quickly to my one night of lust in recent memory, that Thursday before Christmas, and thought, what awful irony: to be pregnant because of a fit of drunken seasonal sentimentality the night before David Blake and I took a last sober look at our ailing five-year-old relationship and agreed to put it out of its misery. Then I thought, Dee Street, you're jumping the gun. You can't even remember how much time has to pass before you can take one of those tests.

In my neighbourhood you can buy second-hand books easier than you can buy tissues or tablets, never mind home pregnancy tests, so I had to wait until I got to Camden Town, where my office is, before going into a chemist's shop. I was pushing open the door of the Boots on the High Street when I recognised coming towards me the bundled-up figure of Theresa O'Connor, friend and, until she'd been tempted away by the offer of a partnership in another solicitors' practice, colleague. She'd had her share of was-she or wasn't-she traumas in the time I'd known her. If she had time for a coffee, perhaps . . .

So engrossed was she in her thoughts, however, and so oblivious to the street life she was walking through, that when I spoke her name it had the effect of saying 'boo' in a dark spooky room.

Hand over heart, she laughed.

So did I. 'You sleepwalking on this side of town for a reason, my dear?'

'Interviews,' she smiled, now recovered. 'Witnesses.' An aggressive passer-by bumped into her and pushed her towards me. Ignoring him she said into my ear, 'Does the name Gerard Ryan ring a bell?'

It was only vaguely familiar but as Theresa's small firm was increasingly specialising in Irish political cases, there wasn't much risk in guessing. 'That alleged senior IRA explosives guy they picked up?'

Her nod 'yep' was full of pride.

3

'You have time for a coffee?'

She shook her head 'nope', pointed to her gloved wrist – 'I'm late as it is. Lunch? Next week? Wednesday?' – and when I said Wednesday would be fine, kissed me on either cheek and was gone.

I bought the kit in Boots and calculated that I couldn't use it until Tuesday.

Four days.

Anything could happen in four days.

There was no message from Gillian Shiraz in the office nor did she ring during the half hour I was there. Neither, fortunately, did anyone else and I got through a lot of work. Then, donning external layers once more, I ventured out into the ominous first spits of thin snow and hailed a taxi.

Between Camden Town and King's Cross a flurry developed and traffic began to back up, which was how it stayed the entire length of Gray's Inn Road, across Holborn, down Fetter Lane and up Fleet Street. By the time the driver pulled an impatient U-turn behind St Clement Dane's church and braked at the kerb just down from the High Court buildings, it was past ten.

As I paid and was stepping out into what was now chilled drizzle I saw my barrister huddled inside the base of the gothic arch that forms the court entrance, gazing up into the sky. Adjusting my coat collar against the weather, I lifted a gloved hand into the air and yelled hello.

Two men in dark topcoats twenty yards ahead turned at my call and I recognised the beaky profile and permed curls of the solicitor acting for my client's ex-husband. I'd never met Tonio Shiraz – had no desire to meet him after all I'd heard about his moodiness and fits of temper – but when the other man raised his hand to his brow as a visor I knew at once that's who he was: only an importer of middle eastern goods would wear a heavy gold bracelet so unselfconsciously into a British court. His solicitor whispered into his ear, which made him scowl at me before they both turned away and continued into the buildings.

My barrister Eleanor had started walking towards me and, when we met up, leaned down from her five foot ten and a half inches to touch her lips to my cheek. She'd spent the middle two weeks of January travelling around the Caribbean and was looking disgustingly tan and blonde.

She smiled as she straightened. 'Well?'

I shook my head. 'You've looked inside?'

She nodded.

I glanced at my watch, then at the busy pavement, then back at my watch. 'Five minutes,' I said.

She shrugged 'sure' and went on inside to wait in the warmth.

The five minutes passed. Gillian Shiraz, I thought, what are you doing? This is not the way to fight for your daughter.

I gave her five more. Eleanor reappeared. 'Dee,' she said, putting her hand on my shoulder.

I sighed a resigned sigh and followed her in.

As we wound our way along corridors and up stairways to one of the modern wings, we reviewed our position and when we reached the area outside Court 37, went straight over to the ex-husband, his solicitor and counsel. 'Our client has been unavoidably detained,' Eleanor started after the introductions.

Shiraz muttered 'I knew it'.

She ignored him. 'What we'd like is a short adjournment. As early as possible next week will be fine.'

'Where is she?' the other barrister wanted to know.

'That is – ah – confidential, I'm afraid.'

The three men looked at each other and you could almost reach out and touch the message passing between them: they intended to refuse but were about to make us grovel for ten minutes before doing it. We deprived them of that small satisfaction at least.

At ten-thirty we filed into the courtroom and took our places along the benches. Everyone stood as the judge entered, then sat down again while the usher called the case on. At that point Eleanor once more rose to her feet.

'If it please your lordship, I have an application to make on behalf of the respondent mother. I have discussed this outside with my learned friend. I am applying for an adjournment of the custody hearing because the respondent is unable to be here today. My client's main witness, Miss Annie Murphy, whose affidavit is filed with the court, was herself called away earlier this week on a personal matter and I believe my client may be with her at this moment. The child whose custody is in dispute is aged two and a half and has lived with her mother since birth. There is no suggestion that if the case were adjourned for a brief period it would in any way prejudice the child's welfare.'

The judge interrupted. 'I have read the affidavits.' He turned to the barrister for the other side. 'Is there an objection to this application?'

The man rose. 'There is, your lordship.'

'Let me hear it please.'

Eleanor sat down.

The other barrister said, 'My lord, with all due respect, the fact of the matter is that the mother has not appeared for this morning's hearing and despite the excuses her own counsel clearly has no idea where she is. For all anybody knows the respondent may have removed the child from the jurisdiction of this court.

'This behaviour is characteristically irresponsible. It serves to reinforce what we contend in our evidence, namely that the respondent, my client's ex-wife, is an unfit mother. She has, if I might remind your lordship, become a lesbian.' He curled the 'l' around his tongue and let the word unfurl. 'She moreover has no fixed address. She and the child spend their nights – long, cold winter nights – *camping* in the open. And not even in an authorised site, but in a so-called women's 'peace' camp' – it was almost 'piss' the way he pronounced it – 'a place completely without facilities, where they are trespassing on Ministry of Defence land, and where their only shelter is an unhealthy, unhygienic plastic tent.

'The applicant, by contrast, owns his own house, earns a good living and has remarried. His present wife does not work outside the home and their domestic circumstances are tranquil and secure. Since discovering last summer the circumstances in which his daughter lives, the applicant has attempted to make several generous contributions towards her welfare and maintenance. When these were thwarted he resorted to channelling small payments through his mother, who keeps in regular contact with her granddaughter. It is his view that the child's well-being – emotional as well as physical – is in serious jeopardy. Because of his concern, which I would suggest is well-founded, I request from your Lordship an immediate order that the child be returned to the court and put into the care of either her father, the applicant hereon, or her paternal grandmother until whatever future date my lord determines.'

The judge turned to Eleanor. 'What do you have to say to that?'

She stood. 'I would first refer your lordship to the evidence concerning the applicant's history of domestic violence. My client divorced him for that reason and has had sole care of her daughter since her birth. The child's father expressed no interest in even seeing her until seven months ago. Might I also refer your lordship to the affidavit of the witness Annie Murphy, the woman alleged by the applicant to be the 'lover' of his ex-wife. Miss Murphy denies that she is now or ever has been homosexual. She explains that she lives in a small room in the residential suburbs of the town of Moleham which she made available to Gillian Shiraz and her daughter six months ago *precisely* to spare them staying out overnight during bad weather. She states in addition that it is her opinion, as a qualified nurse, that the child is fit, healthy and developing perfectly normally for her age. In short, my lord, I would submit that the applicant is over-reacting to a simple request for a short adjournment. Unless I can assist your lordship further . . .'

The judge indicated that he'd heard enough and everyone sat while he shuffled through the evidence, pausing to examine individual documents. Finally after two or three minutes he looked up.

'This hearing is adjourned for three weeks. In the meantime I order that the child should be returned to the court and placed in the care and control of her paternal grandmother.'

I try not to dwell on bad judgments but I couldn't seem to push from my mind the image of what was going to happen: the court official, inevitably a stern young man in a suit, arriving at Gillian's tent and demanding the child Katy; mother and daughter tightening that grip they kept on each other's hands; the tears and screams as the fingers were prised apart and the girl was taken away. The thought distressed me so much I began to feel a little sick, and the sensation grew when I remembered its other possible cause.

The cure, I decided as I stomped my boots on the mat in the office foyer, was a cup of peppermint tea and a conversation with Suze Aspinall, my partner in Aspinall Street (Solicitors) of Camden, and old friend. The question was, would I be so lucky? Once upon a time we'd have automatically had lunch together if neither of us was in court, but since she'd been elected to her local council in a by-election the year before and switched to working flexible part-time hours, catching her had turned into a serendipitous thing. We'd scarcely socialised outside the office either the past few months.

I entered hopefully nevertheless and, tea made, tapped on her door. A laugh familiar but not hers came from the other side and Suze called out for me to come in. She was standing beside her desk, doing up the buttons of her imitation Burberry. Waiting for her, and dressed in what I had no doubt was the real thing, was our colleague of two months, Nicola Steyning. Hope vanished.

'You're just off then?' I said a bit unnecessarily.

Suze grinned her wide grin and nodded as she started pushing her thick, dark shoulder-length hair into her wool hat.

Nicola, six inches taller than either of us and angular as a colt, repeated the noise that passed for a laugh but was closer to a bray. 'Dee *darling*, we're being interviewed,' she said, ' – on the *radio* – a friend – do you know Melissa Curtis? We were at Cambridge together – she's doing a feature on women in the legal profession.'

My 'oh', I'm afraid, was subdued. I wanted to like Nicola Steyning – had been eager to like her ever since Suze's first enthusiastic mention of her after one of our other four associates resigned. She'd sounded so ideal: there was scarcely a worthy cause she hadn't been involved in, from anti-apartheid to homelessness to the transporting of nuclear waste; she'd spent ten years as a local councillor – that's how Suze had met her: she'd been Suze's mentor – and, boon of boons, she had a background in property conveyancing, that boring but lucrative bread and butter service our accountant had been urging us to offer.

At the interview I'd found her too stage-managed by some inner director with a fondness for ham, but that alone didn't explain the antipathy. I had my share, after all, of English friends whose Englishness had inflated into self-parody over the years.

So what was it about her then? Was it that I didn't believe her claim that she'd abandoned her efforts to be nominated for a parliamentary seat? I mean, she was only thirty-eight; for a politician that's early infancy. Or was it simply that she seemed a little too pleased with how right-on she was?

If only I could air my disquiet to Suze like I normally would; if only Suze weren't so overawed by her.

A small inner voice whispered back, You're just jealous, but I shushed it.

Suze's hat was on and she was frowning at me. 'You look a bit ill, Dee, you OK?'

I blamed my expression on the Shiraz decision, which I told them about. Nicola's grimace put capitals on her look of complete and utter disgust and she launched into an anecdote about the campaign she'd run back in '84 that had been about exactly this subject. Suze's frown deepened and she nodded a few times but in the first pause it was me she spoke to. 'I'd offer to drive you to the camp, Dee, but I'm up to my eyeballs in meetings all this afternoon and I've got to leave for a conference at six.' She patted me on the shoulder. 'I hope you find her.'

The mist of mixed emotions dispersed. Of course: I had to find Gillian. I had to prepare her, make sure she co-operated.

'I've got a car,' said a voice behind me. I turned to look at my secretary of three weeks, Claudine Jones, who was standing in the interconnecting doorway, wobbling ever so slightly on the four-inch heels that made her almost as tall as Nicola, and clutching a stack of files to her chest. The long batwing jumper that stopped about three inches from the hem of her short leather skirt was a pure turquoise, a colour that always seems to be wearing *me* if I try it; set against the dark brown of her skin, it vibrated.

I glanced back and forth between her and Suze. 'I can take the train,' I assured them both. 'I always do.' I'd given up my car, and as it turned out, driving, ten years before when I'd moved into my flat on Lisson Place, off the Marylebone Road, and discovered that the Council sold four thousand residents' parking permits for a thousand spaces.

Claudine demonstrated the quality that had made me hire her over an older more experienced rival: she opened her eyes wide and said, 'But I've never *been* to one of those peace camps.'

I changed my mind about the lift.

The vehicle that had been temporarily entrusted to Claudine by her older brother was, from the outside, an unprepossessing six-year-old matt black Renault. Inside it was upholstered in fake leopard fur and the engine that started with the turn of the key had been transplanted from a dead BMW. Given how late we were in setting off, that we stopped to change clothes, and that we got stuck in outbound Friday afternoon traffic on the Westway, we made good time, reaching the Moleham suburbs in under two hours. The house where Gillian's friend Annie Murphy had her room was out here, on a tree-lined street about five miles east of the local American missile base and of the women's peace camp that was next to it. Today the trees stood skeletal against the dark clouds closing in around the afternoon.

As Claudine pulled up to the kerb, I looked over at the decaying three-storey house that a hundred years ago had been built for some prosperous Victorian family. No lights were on, but that didn't mean much: Annie's room was at the back.

I got out of the car and crossed the road. Claudine locked up and followed.

We climbed the four or five steps to the front door, where I reached out and pushed the unmarked bottom bell. Claudine and I listened. All was quiet.

She looked through the letter slot: nothing.

She pressed the bell again and flapped her arms against the February chill. 'I can't *believe* they live outside in *this*,' she said.

I smiled. 'But this is a mild dry day.'

She groaned as if to say, 'Tell me another one' and bent to press her ear to the letterbox. 'I think I heard a creak,' she mumbled. 'Yes. Yes – there it is again.' She stood upright.

I bent to have a listen, then pushed the flap in and put my mouth to the hole. 'Annie? Gillian? It's me – Dee,' I called.

Nothing.

Claudine gave the bell another long press.

There was more creaking but that was all.

'You wait here,' I said. 'I'll check the back.' Descending the steps in a hurry, I crossed the path with equal haste and, when I got to the wooden gate, gave it a push. It yielded and I went on through, past the line of dustbins and around to the rear, where I stood and stared up at the dark first-floor windows. There was a rickety external staircase, left over from the days when this concrete and bramble yard had been a garden, and I thought, better try everything. As a tendency to vertigo is one of my better kept secrets. I clung to the railing and ascended with considerable caution. The door at the first landing was locked but the window adjacent was open, its curtains flapping outside. I didn't bother leaning over, knowing it would be useless – the window was too far away to see into for anyone under seven feet five. Anyway, I had established what I had come to establish: neither of them was here.

Around at the front Claudine had been trying the other buttons and, just as I returned to her side and was stooping for one last peer through the letterbox, the door opened about an inch. Through the crack I distinguished a bald head, a face lined by seventy-some years, hunched shoulders, a cane; what I could make out of the jawline for some reason made me think: if he were a dog he'd be a Corgi. 'We've come to see Annie Murphy – upstairs,' I said. 'We want to leave her a message.'

He sighed, greatly put out, and in case I didn't appreciate how put out, he clicked his tongue a couple of times. He finished up, however, pulling back the door for me.

Only then did he notice Claudine.

A cold green light seemed to come on behind his eyes and I could feel his slack muscles begin shaking in an effort to regroup against the door. I took hold of the edge and kept it open while she slipped past. Inside, she looked right into his face, formed her mouth into a terribly polite smile, and said, 'Thank you.'

He stepped back, as if stunned by her command of English.

The stairs were lit by a 40-watt bulb on a 20-second time switch that left you groping half way up. Very little light made it through the dirty window on the landing beside the phone, which was dangling off the hook. This didn't surprise me. I'd tried the number half a dozen times before we'd left London and finally an operator had told me it was out of order; it was out of order at least every other time I dialled it. But when I picked it up I discovered it was humming the impatient whine of a living line and set it back on the pay box.

We turned down the corridor and made our way to the end door. I knocked.

Nothing. No sound; no reply.

I felt in my pockets. 'Did you bring a pen?'

Claudine reached over, gripped the door knob and twisted her wrist. The door opened.

She looked at me. I looked at her.

I saw complete faith, deference – anxiety.

I felt an upsurge of nerve and, pushing the door back, went in. It was a long rectangular room that, judging from the high ceiling, had been hacked out of a much grander space. The entrance was at the end used for TV watching and entertaining and the eyes of several stuffed animals gleamed from among the plastic bricks as the dim light from the hall fell across them. The other end, just discernible in the gloom, was foreshortened by a divider screen, put there to separate the sleeping area.

I found the light switch and pressed but nothing happened.

Claudine took a step in behind me and hugged herself against a shiver. 'It's freezing in here,' she said.

I pointed to the open window and the blowing curtains I'd seen from outside.

She peered after my finger but followed it upward. 'Look,' she said, 'there's no bulb in that fixture hanging from the ceiling.' She glanced down. 'Is that glass do you think on the floor? And look at the way that screen is tilted.' It was angled our way as if it had been pushed from the other side. A chair piled with clothes had evidently stopped it from falling over.

We both moved towards this as if we were being pulled but were resisting. I thought *Raped*, and then I thought, *Don't think that*.

Claudine got to the screen first and looked. Immediately she clasped her hands across her stomach and glanced away. 'Oh God,' she mumbled.

I reached her side.

A woman was lying front down on the floor, her head by our feet, the 20s style bowl cut of her hair calling the eye to the nape of her neck and the impossible way it was bent.

Annie Murphy.

I too glanced away.

II

I left Claudine sitting, head bowed, on the sofa in Annie's room while I went to put in a 999 call which I have no memory of making but must have made because the next thing I knew the hallway was revolving in a shimmy of flickering yellow light. A moment later men with white jackets sticking out beneath overcoats were brushing past me, trailed by two young police officers.

No longer were we allowed to be inarticulate with feeling: explanations had to be given, notes had to be taken, an accident report had to be filled out, though they did permit us to tell our story with our backs to the business taking place around Annie's body. They were also kind enough to let us in on the initial impression of the doctor who'd arrived with the ambulance. He thought she'd probably climbed up on the old wooden highchair found overturned beside her in order to change the bulb, hadn't stabilised it properly or was just too heavy for it, and had had the ill luck to land at an unfortunate angle. In his opinion she'd been lying there since early that morning – ten or twelve hours. My worry was that it might be another ten or twelve before we'd be out of there, but in fact they weren't inclined to detain us. I checked my watch while Claudine was parking the car on the grass verge opposi⹁ the side gate of Moleham Air Base and was surprised to discover only an hour and a half had passed.

We walked separately across the deserted unlit country road, each at our own pace, and dark as it was out there, and insalubrious, it was still a relief to be in the fresh air. Claudine had been stunned because it was the first time in her life she'd seen a dead body. I hadn't told her, but I wasn't sure a few experiences made a whole lot of difference.

I hooked my fingers into the mesh of the twelve-foot-high perimeter fence, pressed my nose through a hole, and stared out into the night. On the horizon beyond the inner coil of six-foot razor wire only distant blinking lights were visible. Another spot and maybe I'd have taken them for stars. There I knew they were probably from the disco at the barracks.

A searchlight flared out abruptly from the depths of the murk, up and to our right, illuminating as it swept past a pair of soldiers in jungle camouflage gear, rifles resting on their shoulders, walking in my direction. Only the fact that they were inside the razor wire rather than between the two fences told me that they were American not British.

Claudine reappeared at my side. 'It's so vast,' she started, 'I had no idea . . .'

But the soldiers had drawn level with us and one now leered at her and growled, 'Here pussy pussy, nice pussy.' He was black too, but some kind of southern and en route, I could only presume, from unemployment to the Dream.

Claudine muttered, 'Jesus,' and turned away in disgust.

I filled with a hard anger which swelled when I had a sudden vision of Annie Murphy's impossible neck. It was completely irrational, of course: she'd been a peace woman, committed to non-violence, opposed to everything these two ignorant pigs represented, but her death was nothing to do with them. Nevertheless I heard myself yelling back at him anyway, shouting at him not to be such an asshole.

He laughed. The white guy with him found me uproariously funny as well and gave me the finger.

Claudine spoke beside my ear. 'Didn't you say something in the car about a cup of tea?'

I took a long and very deep inhalation. 'Sorry,' I said.

'Why?' she smiled.

We moved away from the fence and continued over the frozen ground, across the gravel drive and onwards another couple of hundred yards in the direction of the copse that partly shielded the camp site from the road. A large fire was recovering under a fresh deposit of fuel and the air smelled of wet wood and stew.

Although distinguishing faces behind all the scarves and hats was impossible, I thought I recognised a ground-length crocheted poncho and made towards its wearer, who was standing, back towards me, in the makeshift kitchen area upwind of the smoke. She turned out however to be a Viennese woman newly arrived with a group of visiting supporters from Austria, Switzerland and Germany, and while in her short time there she'd mastered the secrets of the local tea ritual, she hadn't yet met any of the people I knew.

The next form I tried was also a newcomer (from Brittany), and the woman after her, though only up from Plymouth, didn't recognise any of the names I mentioned. I was glancing around, waiting for the next likely person to emerge, when hands grasped me from behind on either shoulder and a voice deep with the syrup of plums said into my ear, 'I hope this is fake fur. I don't speak to people who wear the skins of endangered blue smoos.'

I turned around, laughing. Evelyn Weaver Clarke was in her usual tweed suit and sturdy brown shoes, her white hair tucked up under a dark wool bobble hat the same nondescript colour as her scarf and mittens. 'Blue *smoos?*'

When she smiled as she was smiling now she looked closer to forty than sixty. She tapped her forehead. 'I've got them on the brain. It's my grandson. He's been making me read him this book his father brought him from New York.'

'Does this mean his father has forgiven you?'

The smile widened; the age dropped to thirty-five. 'His wife has persuaded him that I'm simply going through an eccentric grief response, because of Charles' death.' She looked at Claudine. 'Charles was my husband. He was a banker. So is my son, who is embarrassed to have a mother who stays at a peace camp.'

I introduced the two of them and when that was done said to Evelyn, 'I'm looking for Gillian.'

One brow lifted. 'Goodness, that young Annie hasn't finally persuaded her through the fence?'

The light, jolly way she pronounced the name almost provoked me into telling her about the scene we'd just left, and it would have been easy enough, after all. Comforting too. If Gillian was around, though, she had to be the first to know, so I merely shook my head. 'Do I take it you haven't seen her today?'

'You do,' she said; but then, frowning: 'Someone mentioned something – now who was it . . . ? Ah – of course – it must have been Val.' She pointed into the darkness in the direction opposite the one we'd come from. 'She went to collect firewood oh, I should say about quarter of an hour ago.'

'Thanks,' I said, giving her hand a squeeze before I turned away to say let's go to Claudine. I felt a tap on the shoulder and turned back. Evelyn was holding out a flashlight. I thanked her again.

We picked our way along the path between the fence and the woods, pausing every now and again so Claudine could look at the web patterns woven into the mesh with yarn and at the pictures, most either by or of children, hung here and there. It must have been twenty minutes before I thought I saw a white spot moving around in the gloom ahead. 'Val,' I called out to it. 'Val.'

It moved upwards, stopped, held, then began to come our way. We met up near the black plastic rubbish bag she was filling with wood and, after we'd exchanged a hug, she pulled her earmuffs off over her spiky tangle of white-blonde hair. A dozen pierced earrings dangled along the outer rim of her left ear, like so many crystals off a tilted chandelier; between the mere hoop and stud on her right was tattooed the black and yellow symbol for radiation. She was my height, about five foot two, but about half my dress size, her skinniness emphasised by the black leggings and black leather motorcycle jacket she lived in. She was probably two thirds my age, a year or two older than Annie, a year or two younger than Gillian.

Our arrival gave her an excuse to have a cigarette, which she rolled without removing her black fingerless gloves while Claudine and I parked ourselves on a couple of nearby rocks. When she'd lit up and savoured the first bite of smoke, she looked down at me and said, 'It's Gillian, isn't it? She bottled out.'

I nodded.

'Shit,' she said, hacking at the soil with the toe of her Doc Marten.

'How did you guess?'

She kicked the bag of wood closer to our rocks and sat herself down facing us. 'If you want to know the truth I think I probably knew when I saw her driving away yesterday afternoon. I told myself she must be on her way to London but I don't think I really quite believed it.'

'Why?'

She shrugged. 'Because of the state she's been in about Annie.'

'Tell me about that.'

'But you know – surely . . .'

'All I know is I have a missing client.'

Val started with Monday lunchtime, when Gillian had arrived back from Moleham muttering irritably about how Annie had left Katy at the doctor's by herself after offering to stay with her while Gillian was at the dole office sorting out the cock-up over her last benefit cheque. Questioning established that a receptionist *had* been looking after Katy, who was happy and unharmed, and that Annie had left a note saying something urgent had come up and she'd be back as soon as possible.

As Gillian knew Annie was due out on an agency nursing assignment the next morning, she had assumed 'soon' meant that day. When Annie hadn't returned by late Tuesday afternoon, Gillian's anxiety set in.

'Wednesday when I bumped into her she'd just spoken to you – said you'd told her that if Annie wasn't back by Thursday morning she should start looking everywhere she could think of.'

'I said it to keep her busy as much as anything.'

'Yes – well – it did. She arrived here yesterday first thing looking red and puffy around the eyes, dropped Katy off at the playgroup, borrowed some money for petrol and was gone, I don't know, I'd say about four hours, till lunchtime. When she came back she wasn't weepy any more, she was pissed off: how could Annie put her through this and how could she call herself a friend and how when she saw her again she'd be telling her x, y, and z. It was all understandable but my God was it over the top.' She sucked on her cigarette and, discovering it had gone out, began to fumble in the pocket of her jacket. 'Then she started comparing Annie to Mary.'

'Who's Mary?' Claudine asked.

'Her ex-lover,' Val said.

Claudine looked at me. ' "Lover"? But the brief said . . .' She frowned. 'Isn't it part of your custody defence for Gillian that she isn't gay?'

I shook my head. 'No. All we're saying is that she hasn't been in a lesbian relationship with Annie Murphy, which is what her ex-husband's chosen to allege. It's Annie he's wrong about.'

As Claudine was contemplating this piece of information, Val went on: 'Anyway, when she began making out that she was being "abandoned" yet again, that was it. I knew how worried she was about facing her ex-husband in court and losing Katy but I couldn't keep my mouth shut. I told her I didn't think that was quite fair – reminded her what a good friend Annie has been to her – and she took it wrong, instantly went all prickly like Cancers can, you know? – as if now *I* was letting her down – and went off in a huff.'

'And you haven't seen her since?'

'No, I saw her again about half an hour later, after she came back from checking Annie's room one last time and phoning you.'

'She told you she spoke to me?'

'She told me she was going to. Didn't she?'

'Nope.'

She thought a moment. 'Well she was only gone about as long as it takes to drive to the house, do some short business and drive back. I was in the field on the other side of the gate catching up on the gen about the council's latest tactic to get us out of here when her car drove past. By the time I got out of the conversation, she'd fetched Katy and was throwing their sleeping bags and cooking things into the back seat. She saw me walking towards her, I know she did, but she got in and drove off.'

She'd found her lighter but couldn't get it to work. She threw the cigarette on the ground. 'What'll they do to her?'

'The tipstaff –'

'The what?'

'The court official – the tipstaff – he's on his way here even as we speak with an order for her to hand Katy over.'

She sighed from way down low. 'Oh dear.'

I leaned across and put my hand over hers. 'There's worse news than that I'm afraid. We've just come from Annie's.'

.   *   *   *

18

I'm used to the three flights of steps up to my flat and while I don't normally take them at a run, neither do I generally lumber. That evening after Claudine dropped me off, however, I felt as if my jeans had been dipped in cement and cleats attached to the soles of my wellingtons. When I'd pumped my way to the second landing, the walls suddenly began to rotate and my face felt so hot I yanked off my hat and scarf. As I grabbed hold of the railing with both hands, the image of Annie materialised in front of me – that neck, those eyes, that startled 'o' of a mouth – and I thought, I'm going to faint. Somehow I managed not to.

I also managed to force myself up the last flight and, once home, stripped down to tights and sweatshirt, decanted a generous measure of brandy into a glass, and after a quick random check of the plants that occupied every flat surface and hung in front of every light source to make sure they hadn't dried out, wrapped myself in the thick blanket I'd picked up on a holiday in Morocco and curled into the armchair beside the heater. The chair had been one of David's spots and when the alcohol had warmed away the queasiness and obliterated Annie's ghost, it seemed to me I could almost feel him there again, long and sprawled out, baggy in his aged corduroys and shapeless green sweater, his silver brown hair just that bit too long, the way he let it go in winter.

Suddenly it was four Februaries earlier and we were lying curled up around each other in a kingsize bed under a huge feather quilt, staring out at the rain falling on the bay in Portree, on the Isle of Skye. His wife had been dead about eight months and in the aftermath of her murder his confidence in his judgment, especially about people, had been up-ended, affecting his work as a psychiatrist particularly badly. Raised as he had been to bear up, he'd seemed, of course, to be handling it: he consulted one of his colleagues at the hospital a few times, began to wave a few technical terms over himself and finally proclaimed, abracadabra, that the worst was over. Simultaneously, however, he abandoned the plans he'd been nurturing to open a new hostel for young schizophrenics, sold his home and dropped out of the political activities that had taken up most of his free time for twenty-odd years. He had reasons for each decision, quite unrelated to what he'd been through, but I couldn't help feeling nevertheless that he still really wasn't at all sure that he could trust himself.

Skye was a place where he'd had memorable times as a boy; the way he imagined it we would go and we would walk ten or fifteen miles a day and it would be good for us. Instead, we'd hardly left the bed except to bathe and go out for food. As a result I'd run out of that quintessentially a-romantic but indispensable item, spermicidal jelly, on the Saturday night – but while I panicked, he suddenly started saying so what about the cream, maybe we should have a child. I was dismissive: the firm's finances as usual were precarious, and when I thought of my friends who were juggling careers and motherhood they seemed to me to be inhabiting some new chamber of hell. I had no desire to join them, and as he didn't push it, that was that.

Six or eight months later when we'd borrowed that garish flat of his niece's ex-husband's sister in Marbella and recommenced epic lovemaking, I discovered a small tear in my diaphragm. Again he'd raised the subject of having a child and again I'd drawn his attention to the practical realities.

That was the last time we'd had a holiday and the last time we'd discussed the subject.

What, I wondered, would he do if he learned I might be pregnant now? Would he consider coming back to London?

No, that was ridiculous – as ridiculous as the idea that I might move up north. I'd been brought up in LA, for pity's sake; I might enjoy being foreign in a cosmopolitan city like London, but in a provincial Yorkshire mining village where I'd always be the outsider, that American woman, the doctor's 'missus' . . . ? His attitude – that it would be fine if I gave it a chance, that I would find work, might even found another firm – it was based on pure fantasy. It ignored a significant little detail of reality: me.

I opened my eyes. Dammit, I was doing it to myself again. I had to stop it – had to keep reminding myself about those three days between now and the test.

Three whole days.

I pushed myself up out of the chair. What I needed to do was take them one hot bath at a time.

A conference and a dinner party kept me occupied that Saturday, and on Sunday I went to visit friends in Brighton. Because I didn't feel actively sick either morning, I told myself I didn't feel sick at all. I left the answerphone on every time I went out and checked it immediately every time I came back in, but Gillian didn't get in touch.

Most of Monday I was in court and when I got back to the office, Claudine looked up from her typing and took out the earpiece of the dictaphone. 'One of the policemen who interviewed us at Annie's on Friday was here this morning,' she said. 'The inquest is tomorrow and he needed to clear up a few points for his accident report.'

'He came up from Moleham to do that? Why didn't he just phone?'

'I wondered that too. Remember the old boy who let us in to the house? Well it seems he's been going around saying it wasn't really an accident at all . . .'

'Oh for . . . that doctor at the scene *said*. . .'

'They know, they know. But the guy belongs to some citizens group – knows the chief constable – so they're having an autopsy done at the lab in Scotland Yard to keep him happy.'

'Yes – well – that "citizens group" must be the Masons,' I muttered.

'The who?'

If there had been time I would have gone back to the twelfth century, the Knights Templar and the invention of commercial credit. Instead I just said, 'The Masons; they're a male secret society. They swear oaths of brotherhood and learn various palm greasing rituals. Is he coming back?'

She shook her head. 'He seemed to think my answers would do.' She handed me a pile of letters to sign.

'And Gillian?' I asked. 'Any word?'

But she just shook her head again.

That night at three I woke up with a start out of a suffocating dream and no matter what I counted or what breathing exercises I tried from bygone yoga classes, I couldn't get back to sleep. It felt ominous to me, and so it was to prove. I found myself heading in to work that Tuesday morning with my fingers crossed, so fervently was I wishing that Suze and her ear would be in and available. As I struggled up Parkway against the wind, however, I spotted her in the distance tilting it towards Nicola Steyning, who was pushing open the door of the Favourite Café; by the time their laughter reached me, they were inside.

I arrived at my desk in such a grumpy mood that I should actually have cancelled all my appointments in order not to inflict myself on anyone else. Trouble was, I felt so mean I didn't think of that until I ended up facing the one kind of client I felt least able to accommodate, the type that is to a lawyer what a hypochondriac is to a GP. Gold and silk decorated her frame in the way plastic and wool-blend decorated mine, and from her sculpted coiffure to her elaborate make-up to her perfectly manicured nails she was a study in under-occupied self-indulgence.

How in God's name had she heard about us? Were we this fashionably déclassé? And why did this sort of woman invariably induce a sudden pang of doubt in me about sisterhood?

As she talked on at me I recrossed my legs and shifted around the other way in my chair. But it was no good; I couldn't concentrate. Not now that I knew.

I was pregnant.

For sure.

The little pink dot had materialised on the white square of paper from the home tester kit in ten minutes, just like the instructions said would happen if the results were positive.

His seed. My egg.

A hit.

'. . . I want to sue for defamation,' she was insisting in her over-acted rendition of an upper class accent. 'I see no reason why I should stand for such . . .'

I nodded absently.

And what was more, no Gillian. *Still*.

The client stopped speaking and stared at me expectantly.

'Excuse me?' I said.

'I said I'm so pleased you feel you can help.'

I frowned at her. 'I don't think I said that.' I stood up. 'I'm far too busy.' I put out my hand. 'Sorry.'

Her expression dropped from pouting and slightly flirtatious into displeased and aggrieved. One side of her lip lifted just so, becoming almost a sneer as she leaned forward to convey what promised to be something sharp and high handed. Just as she opened her mouth to deliver it, however, the telephone rang.

'It must be an emergency for me to be interrupted by a call,' I smiled, taking the opportunity to show her to, and through, the door. But my smugness wasn't to last.

It was the duty solicitor from the Magistrates' Court in Moleham. 'I'm telephoning on behalf of Mrs Gillian Shiraz,' he said. 'She's asked me to inform you that she's just been charged with the manslaughter of Miss Annie Murphy.'

Two

Someone is speaking into my ear in a low voice – a woman – and I'm so entranced by the rhythm of her speech it doesn't matter that I don't understand a word. I open my eyes to slits and, as I do, a face looms up beyond the end of my nose and peers in at me. It is lit eerily by a flashlight with weak batteries and I flinch away.

Cool fingers press my forehead, encircle my wrist, count my pulse, let go. Other hands slip under my arms and half push, half lift, my torso to an upright sitting position. I'm a dead weight even to myself, however; unsupported I flop back down like a puppet whose strings have just been cut. There's urgent whispering and the hands push me back up.

I've definitely been drugged.

The low voice speaks again in my ear and this time I comprehend the single word 'sorry'. The next moment a musty woollen hat like a balaclava but without the holes is pulled over my face.

'Cut it out,' I start, sounding like a 45 at 33⅓, but even while I'm struggling to marshal my energy in protest, a gag is being tied around my mouth.

My back is pushed, my ankles are pulled and a lot of grunting and heaving goes on, but when my feet finally touch ground my legs won't hold. The whispering now has an exasperated tone and the hands that shove themselves under my arms this time don't do it gently. The other person lifts my ankles and the two of them scoot with me quickly over what seems quite a distance. Finally my ankles are set down, a key is put in a lock, a door is opened.

They tilt me, back above feet, and carry me up interminable stairs, open another door, carry me into a room and drop me on a soft bed. A blanket is put over me, the hood and gag are removed.

'Hey,' I try, but even as the rest of the sentence is forming, the low voice is saying something which I decide must mean I am to sleep. In any case as soon as it is said footsteps vibrate across the floor, away from me; the door opens and closes again, a barrel drops in a lock.

I am alone once more.

At first the dark is impenetrable but I make myself stare into it until eventually the shapes begin to distinguish themselves: a bedside table, a chest of drawers, a chair with clothes draped over it. The upright bulbous shape on the table has to be a lamp, and using all the energy I have I push myself into a half sit, bend my arm once, twice, to get it functioning, and reach out. My fingers land on the switch, which I am nearly too feeble to press but finally do, and as my arm drops to the table, exhausted, my little cave fills with light and shadows. The clothing on the chair is revealed as male: jeans, a dark sweatshirt, a pair of white trainers. The table is cluttered with things: a digital clock (it's 3:05), a cassette recorder, a tobacco pouch, a comb, a mug, a plate, two books. I squint. One is the Bible. The other is *A Marx Reader*.

Groucho? Karl? But it's hopeless even trying to lift the book and I drag my hand back. As I do, I notice that my right thumbnail is broken and I spread out my fingers: all the nails are broken and the skin on both the back and the palm is scratched. My other hand is the same.

I push up my sleeves. There are scratches and bruises on both forearms.

I slump back down. I can give in to panic – I'm a hair's breadth away. Or I can refuse.

I've certainly fought it often enough before. In fact, come to think of it, I fought it not that long ago.

I

I hadn't blamed my hormones for my behaviour for at least a

decade but the reorganisation they were going through was the only reason I could think of for the way I was thrown by the news of Gillian's arrest. But while Claudine could get away with crying out 'Manslaughter?' at the top of her range, with protesting 'But it was an accident!' and even with 'But Val saw her drive away the afternoon before!', I was She Who Copes, the owner (at least hypothetically) of an extra layer of skin that I was supposed to slip on like a plastic mac against the rains of angst and trauma. People did not pay me large sums per hour, after all, to watch me transform into Gelatinous Girl.

Fortunately it was late in the afternoon before the police authorities transferred Gillian up to town, by which time I'd purged my emotions in the stack of tedious odds and ends of paperwork that normally bore me into procrastination. Even when Suze put her head around the door and said why didn't I join her and Simone and Nicola for lunch, I stayed put, keeping at it until four, when I left for Holloway Prison.

My secret theory about London's 'facility' for women is that there was a mix-up in the plan chest of the architect who designed it and that no one noticed the mistake until the red brick bottling factory was already halfway up. The resemblance is most obvious from a distance but strikes again as you walk in through the high front gate towards the guards' hut and, that afternoon, seeing a new guard on duty, I made a comment about it as I handed over my letter of introduction. She wasn't the slightest bit amused, however, and examined the typed sheet minutely before pointing me to the adjacent waiting room, where oily markings on the paintwork above most of the moulded plastic chairs spoke of the ten thousand others who must have fretted there over the years.

My wait wasn't all that long in fact as prison waits go; the ten minute minimum had barely passed when another guard appeared to escort me to the corridor of small cells dignified by the name 'solicitors' visits area'. They were all the same – ten-by-eight cubicles containing one wobbly aluminium and formica table, two chairs and an ashtray. The one I was assigned this time also had a small window too high to look through and too dirty to let in sunlight even if there'd been any. It was open and there was no heater, so I kept my coat on as I sat down and let my eyes adjust to the over-bright light from the fluorescent ceiling panels.

The Gillian Shiraz I was there to see was a rounded woman, about five foot five, with a pre-Raphaelite bush of dark shoulder-length hair and a fondness for hippy-reject velvet Sergeant Pepper jackets and long billowing skirts. Even though I'd known her for a couple of years on and off, she still met me with her chin forward and a chip worn like an epaulette on her shoulder and I still had to joke about how uneasy they made me before she'd take off her little round opaque black glasses in the wire granny frames that reflect you back at yourself.

The Gillian Shiraz who was brought in supported between two guards and set into the other chair wasn't wearing the protective glasses, and the watery blue eyes now exposed were rimmed in pink. The hollowness of her cheeks and lankness of her hair were set off by a shapeless black cardigan buttoned askew over a yellowed wrap-around hospital gown.

The sedative they'd given her made her sound like someone just coming round from oral surgery. 'He'sh got her now ashn't he?' she managed.

I sighed. 'Yes. She's at your mother-in-law's.'

She propped her elbows on the table and covered her face with her hands. She was struggling not to break down and I wanted her to succeed.

I said, 'Tell me everything that happened between the time you hung up the phone after talking to me on Wednesday and the time you were arrested.'

She mumbled something into her palms which I couldn't make out.

'I'm sorry?' She raised her head and enunciated the words 'I didn't do it' very deliberately.

I nodded and reached across and set my hand as close to hers as I thought she'd allow. My instinct was to believe her simply because she was so involved in the peace movement; on the other hand, she'd been treated pretty rough by one father and one husband and for all I knew the bottled-up anger she felt about that had somehow come out against Annie.

'About what happened,' I repeated.

She took a deep breath. 'I did what we agreed – tried to put

Annie out of my mind, not worry. I took Katy into the playground in town, then we had chips and visited a couple of friends. They invited us to stay the night and after the kids went to bed we went through a couple of bottles of wine. It was great: I hadn't been drunk in months – months and months – and it was just what I needed. Trouble was, I woke up all dehydrated about five Thursday morning and started worrying about Annie again and couldn't get back to sleep. When Katy woke up I packed her into the car, left her at the playgroup at the camp and went to see if Annie'd come back yet, which she hadn't. I drove around looking for her at every place I could think she might be, then went back to her room . . .'

'What time was that?'

'About one.'

'And?'

'She wasn't there.' She looked at her hands. 'And I thought – such hateful things about her. I – wished her dead. I thought she'd – thought she'd – let me down. And now – now I feel so – so . . .'

'Listen – Gillian – if you're only guilty of bad thoughts, getting you out of here will be a cinch. You were supposed to phone me Thursday afternoon. Was the phone broken?'

She sighed again and shook her head. 'If only it had been.'

'What do you mean?'

'I rang – rang Tonio.'

The groan got out before I could stop it: 'Oh Gillian . . .'

'I know,' she said, biting her lip, 'I know.' She paused until the tears backed down. 'I told him,' she carried on, 'that Annie'd been called away by an emergency. I asked him would he put the hearing off until she got back.'

I had a sudden memory of Tonio Shiraz muttering under his breath outside the courtroom on Friday. No wonder he'd seemed so ready for our adjournment request. 'You didn't seriously think he'd agree, did you?'

'I wasn't thinking, I just knew I couldn't face him in court on my own. I knew you'd say I had to do it and I – I don't know – I guess I was praying he might do the decent thing for once in his life.' She glanced up, towards the window, and I followed her glance. Beyond the bars mouths of black cloud seemed to be devouring brighter lines of overcast sunlight. The weather was building towards one of those end-of-the-world skies.

I decided she was telling the truth. 'And when he didn't?' I prompted.

She looked back at me. 'I started to cry – in fact if you want to know the truth I had hysterics, which he of course loved. He started mocking me, just like he always used to, saying what a walkover it was going to be getting custody of Katy – things like that – and suddenly something in me went bang and I started shouting at him. Told him I'd see him dead first. Threatened to tell the court exactly what a bully he really was – he thought that was *funny*. Anyway, in the end I slammed the phone down on him, grabbed some of Katy's things, rushed back to the camp to collect her and just pointed the car north. I thought about going to a friend in Ireland but I didn't have enough money for the ferry so I headed for Wales instead.'

'Which part?'

'West. Not far from Carmarthen. An old friend of mine lives in a big old sort of communey place – used to be a hotel.'

'And she/he put you up?'

'She – yes. Happily. No questions asked. We stayed there from Thursday night until Sunday afternoon. We'd be there now only I – well – it's so dumb.' She began picking at her fingers.

'Go on.'

It took her several moments before she finally confessed. 'We needed petrol and I only had a fiver left, so I filled up at the garage and – and – just drove away.'

Another groan escaped me but this time she jerked her head up sharply. 'What else was I supposed to do? I couldn't sign on, my friend has no money. I was trying to hold on to my child, for God's sake.'

'I'm not blaming you,' I protested, pleased to see a bit of the old spirit returning even if I didn't much like it snapping at me. 'What's the evidence against you? Have they given you any idea?'

'Yes. The old man who lives downstairs from Annie – the one who's hated us since he found out we're "Moleham women" – he heard me yelling and shouting. The woman next door saw me run away.'

'But those things happened early Thursday afternoon you said. The doctor who came to the scene after we found Annie's body Friday evening said she'd died that morning. That's at least – at least – twelve hours after you left.'

'Ah but Dee, that's not what the autopsy showed. According to the autopsy she died of a broken neck within an hour of the time I was in her room.'

I phoned Moleham police station from a public booth on Holloway Road and rehearsed my client's version of events to the detective superintendent in charge of the case.

He was already familiar with it and feigned a certain tolerant weariness as he told me so. 'Moreover,' he added, 'Mr Tonio Shiraz called in to see us and made no mention of any telephone conversation with his ex-wife.'

'Yes – well – it isn't information he'd volunteer. He's been banned from talking to her. He can be held in contempt of court if he admits it. He must be persuaded to tell the truth.'

He sighed and said he'd get back to me.

Half an hour later, as I was unlocking the inner front door of the firm's now deserted office, the phone started ringing.

'Tonio Shiraz positively denies speaking to his ex-wife.'

I made a sceptical noise.

'But surely what happened is plain enough, Miss Street,' he said, his surprise at my attitude apparently genuine. 'Your client's "friend" Miss Murphy changed her mind about testifying at the custody hearing I understand was due to have taken place on Friday. Your client became enraged. It was a typical, spontaneous crime of passion.'

I pointed out to him that the 'lesbian lovers' picture of things was due to be contested in court but to no avail. Minds were made up in Moleham. I moved on to the mundane. 'Have Annie Murphy's family been informed?' I asked. This was code for 'How long do I have before the media get hold of the story?'

'She was brought up by nuns in a convent school. According to our information there are no living relatives.'

I Slipped into the ladies to wash off the feeling Holloway always leaves me with and found myself standing sideways in front of the full-length mirror thinking, *no family at all – imagine.* And not only Annie but Gillian too, though in her case it wasn't because of death but because her parents had excommunicated her for eloping with a man whose father was half Italian, half Turkish.

I'd asked her, anyway, if she was sure she didn't want me to contact her parents but she'd shrugged and said, 'Why? They don't know I'm divorced or have a child or live at a peace camp, why break the silence by telling them I'm in prison?'

'They'll find out,' I'd pointed out. But she'd just shrugged again.

By comparison I was blessed. My mother had enough of a life of her own not to pass judgment on mine (or not too often at least) and she was living it six thousand miles away, which was a great boon to our rapport. So were her liberal instincts.

Which did not mean I could tell her about my current small problem. She might not be putting pressure on me, but she hoped for a grandchild someday. She might accept the need for legalised abortion in the abstract, but accept the need for her daughter to have one? It was outside her values.

Was it outside mine? That was the question.

My stomach, astonishingly, was still flat and my breasts, aching and lollopy as they felt, looked utterly normal.

I couldn't have it on my own; how could I do that? My one-bedroom place was barely large enough for me, never mind two of us, and it was up all those stairs. If I moved, though, I'd have to buy a place; if I bought a place I'd need a lot more money and the firm was already overstretched with Suze on part-time and Simone due to go on three months' maternity leave followed by at least six months of a three-day week. There was no way I could do it too *and* take a wage increase. Besides, in my uncertain fantasies of myself as a mother, becoming a single one had never figured except as one of the last things I'd want to be.

I remembered what I'd come back to the office for and, returning to my desk, looked up the home number of my semi-retired pathologist friend Dr Mary Mackay. What I wanted from her wasn't the usual second opinion on the police post-mortem conclusions but a second complete autopsy by an independent expert.

'You're in luck, Dee my love,' she said in the rolling Glaswegian accent that twenty years in England had hardly flattened. 'I'm in the Met morgue first thing tomorrow anyway. I'll do a preliminary and give you a ring.'

My next call was to George Appleby, an investigator I'd used when I was trying to discover who really killed David Blake's wife. In fact we'd worked together on lots of cases in the days before women entered the field; now I tended to save him for instances like this, when I needed someone who knew the legal aid expenditure guidelines inside out from long experience and was still willing to work to them from time to time.

I was only three quarters through the story when he interrupted. George can be an impatient bugger when he's decided what you're asking while you're still leading up to it.

'I make it you want three things, Dee my sweet,' he said in his unrepentant smoker's voice. 'You want me to find out what your man Shiraz has been up to lately, and particularly the Thursday afternoon of said Annie Murphy's demise. You want me to snoop around Telecom for confirmation that the Shiraz woman was on the phone she said she was on when she said she was on it. And you probably want me to drive out to Moleham yesterday and interview as many of the neighbours as I can find.'

'Not probably, definitely. Two people witnessed Gillian leaving, *some*body must have seen Annie entering later. I need to know exactly when that was – and if anybody was with her.'

'Your wish is my command,' he said, putting on an upper class voice. Then he reverted to his East End accent. 'I'll aim to get out there tomorrow afternoon.'

It was about ten to nine when I finally got home and after hurriedly scrambling a couple of eggs, making whole-wheat toast and pouring a glass of fresh apple juice, I sat down on the sofa in front of the TV in the sitting room to fortify myself against the impending news broadcast. The lead item was the national round-up of eight alleged members of two mainland IRA cells, which immediately made me think of my friend Theresa. She was busy enough defending one IRA client. If even two more came to her no one would see her again for years.

The next story was about Middle East hostage negotiations, and the one after that reported on the rumour from Geneva about the possible removal of American missiles from Britain. Vacancies in the health service, an impending social services strike, hypothermia statistics, a couple of business items and an anecdote about the Queen Mother followed, and then we were into the weather.

It hadn't been on. I couldn't believe it.

I turned to the nine-thirty radio news and, when it wasn't on there either, calmed myself with a glass of Rioja while I waited for the ITV *News at Ten*. After that I sat through *Newsnight* on BBC2 and, when it again wasn't on, waited up for the radio World Service report at midnight. Only after that had finished did I accept my luck: there hadn't been any reporters at the court when Gillian was charged.

It was a reprieve that might last at best eighteen hours – until the police put out a press release – but it was more than I'd have dared hope for.

I was on my way to bed in this relieved mood when it came to me that there was an angle I'd overlooked. Annie had disappeared for something like three days – she must have stayed with someone. If I could locate whoever that someone was, I might be able to find out exactly when she'd left them to return to her place.

And then I realised there was one person who just might be able to give me a lead.

Because I'd never met Grandmother Shiraz, I started from the assumption that she shared her son's worldview, a probability which, if true, meant that she would refuse even to speak to me on the telephone, never mind agree to admit me to her home. The only way around this that I could think of was to drop in on her unannounced early the next morning – despite the fact that she lived somewhere out in the southernmost reaches of what the boundary setters insist is still London.

After a twenty-minute journey on the tube to Waterloo, a wait of ten minutes, twenty minutes on the train, another ten-minute wait, a fifteen-minute bus ride and a ten-minute walk, most of it uphill in drizzle, I found myself on a street of between-the-wars detached houses in the vicinity of Cannon Hill Common. The one I wanted, number 24, was dark.

I knocked with more confidence than I felt (if Tonio was here I had no idea what I'd say) and at first there was silence; then I heard little footsteps and a little shout, followed by a heavier footfall.

A stout woman with fly-away grey hair pulled back into a bun partially opened the door and looked out at me with suspicion across a shelf of bosom. 'Yes?'

I told her who I was and rushed on like one of those brush salesmen who used to stick their foot in the door when I was a kid: 'I'd like to talk to Katy if that's possible. She knows me. She's been to my office and played with my typewriter and dictaphone, and I've visited her at the camp. I realise this is highly irregular and I understand that your sympathies will be with your son, but I . . ."

Suddenly the door was pulled open a bit further and a quiet two-and-a-half-year-old voice said, 'Hello, Dee.' I looked down into Katy's wide and serious eyes, then squatted to greet her at her own level. She stepped back into her grandmother's skirt and pulled some of the knobbly wool across her face. Her thumb went into her mouth.

I reached over, stroked her almost black hair, tugged one of her pony tails and stood up. (If only I could be sure of having one like Katy . . .) Tonio's mother, now smiling at me, opened the door fully and gestured me in.

'Actually,' she said, 'I think my son has been beastly to Gillian and I have told him so. He spent too much time with his father, that's the trouble with him. The way he's treated Gillian is exactly the way my ex-husband treated me. He never so much as visited his child; never so much as sent her a birthday card, until his new wife started putting pressure on him. And I've said it to him, I've said, Tonio, no matter what you tell me Gillian is, and no matter what they say she's done, she's been a good mother to Katy.' She leaned towards me. 'Between you and me, I'll say something else for her too, she's been very brave. All of them at those peace camps, Greenham and that, they're all brave... Now here, let me take your wet things. You'll catch your death. Would you care for a cup of tea?'

I said I could think of nothing nicer and was led by Katy into the sitting room at the back of the house to wait and warm myself by the newly banked coal fire just catching in the grate. It was a light room in spite of the lowering blackness of the sky visible through the net curtains – light and safely old-fashioned; a room with its heart in the forties. The two armchairs to either side of the fireplace were covered in the same worn floral chintz as the long settee that ran in between them. There was an upright piano against the back wall, with a massive ginger cat asleep on the bench in front of it. A sewing machine stood open on a side table and the TV was concealed beneath a draped cloth. Knick-knacks and framed photos were lined up on the mantelpiece and I noticed a Bible and a few other books, but otherwise every flat surface was occupied by one variety or another of large leafy house plant.

I was admiring the blooms on a Christmas cactus when she reappeared bearing our drinks on a tray. 'They're all so healthy,' I said.

She smiled. 'I throw away the dead ones.'

We talked indoor gardening for a quarter of an hour or so until Katy, who'd been playing with a pile of toys behind her grandmother's armchair, got used to me again – enough so that she started interrupting us with questions and demands and facts about this toy and that to try to get us to turn our conversation her way. We were happy enough to oblige and within a minute or two I was sitting cross-legged on the floor beside her, discussing her collection of plastic farm animals.

'I need to ask you about your trip to the doctor last week, Katy,' I said to her when I thought the moment had come. 'Do you remember that?'

She nodded and held up a giraffe which had strayed mysteriously into the wrong basket. We had a giggle together about that and I reached for one of those horrible adolescent Sindys (in wedding veil, nurse's uniform and red cowboy boots) and an even more horrible and much bigger rubber baby with a nappy snapped on to its hips. 'This,' I said of the Sindy, 'is your mum, and this –' I said of the baby, 'is you.'

She selected a plastic caricature of a car and put it down on the carpet. 'Car,' she said.

I reached towards the toy basket again. 'And who else went with you?'

Her eyes widened. She was mystified.

'Me?' I said. 'No. I was in London. Your gran? ... No, she was at home too.' I danced a cloth doll in front of her and said, 'Who's this?'

She frowned and then, suddenly, was all grin. 'Annie!' she shouted, 'Auntie Annie!' Then she clapped.

Mentally I crossed my fingers and steadied my nerve so I wouldn't scare her off with my excitement. Calmly I piled the dolls on the car. 'Okay, here we are, on our way to town – brmmm, brmmm – and here we are buying petrol – brmmm, brmmm ... did you get petrol?'

'No,' she said.

'Right, OK, we drive along, da-da-te-da – no petrol – past the camp and the trees and ...'

'... and the so-jers with the rye-fells ...'

'Yes, and the big houses ...'

'... and the horrible boys who wee wee'd on our tent ...'

'Yes, and we see the town coming up in the distance ...'

'The town! Hooray! Smarties!'

'Smarties?'

She nodded enthusiastically and got a bit of red lego and held it up to the sucking lips of the baby doll. 'Annie always buys Smarties.'

'Where does she do that?'

'The bacconits,' she said in a tone that ticked off my stupidity.

'I see, so did you go there in the car?'

'Walk there.' (Yes, I was one hell of a dummy.) 'Car stays with mummy at HS'.

I decided this meant they'd parked at the DHSS. I said, 'So you ate the Smarties before you went to the doctor?'

She shook her head and sighed. I'd dropped even more points.

'But you went to the shop?'

She nodded.

'I see... And did you meet anyone there?'

She scowled and reached again for the basket of farm animals. I retrieved the raggedy Annie doll and attempted to retrieve my position. 'OK, here we are again, we leave the tobacconist's and what? Can we walk to the doctor's or do we maybe take a bus?'

She danced a horse and a cow and seemed not to have heard me.

'Katy?' I said. 'Honey?'

'Walk,' she said. I heard petulance.

'Do we talk to anyone on the street?' I persevered. 'Does anyone stop us?'

The scowl returned. 'A course not. It's town. Mummy told me always – mummy said... mummy...' She stopped dancing the animals and stared at the spot on the carpet where they'd been. Her lips began to quiver and big tears began to roll down the side of her nose. 'Mummy,' she repeated.

I reached over and folded her up into my arms.

II

Katy's grandmother let me use her telephone. It was barely 9 am: if I could catch George Appleby before he started his day, I could get him to stop in to the sweet shop today when he went to Moleham to do the interviewing. Whoever'd sold Katy her pack of Smarties there would be one of the last people to have seen Annie Murphy alive. If she was a regular customer, she might even have said something, dropped some clue about where she went after she left Katy at the doctor's. George's answerphone, however, was already on and there wasn't the usual message about trying his bleeper number. When I dialled it I discovered why: his subscription had been suspended for non-payment of bill.

He was having his typical February.

Back at Waterloo Station I tried him one more time on the off-chance, then rang in to the office to let Claudine know I was on my way.

'Take your time,' she said. 'Your two morning appointments have both cancelled.'

I'd hung up and was nearly to the tube entrance before I realised I didn't *need* to suppress my curiosity. Moleham was less than ninety minutes away by train. In an earlier era, when the peace camp there was new and the arrests frequent, I'd even had a commuter railcard. And I was carrying my briefcase – I could get some work done *en route*.

I called Claudine back, said I'd be back by two and asked her to rearrange my lunch date with Theresa. Then I made my way to Paddington, where I arrived five minutes before the next train departed for Moleham.

Because of my many visits to the Magistrates' Court I could set my feet on automatic at the station and know I'd end up there ten minutes later. The DHSS office, I had a vague memory, was somewhere in the same vicinity, but I didn't realise until I found it that it bordered the same square as the courthouse. Now, I thought, looking around, if I remembered rightly – yes, there it was, over on the other side, in front of the town hall: one of those fifties-style mounted maps for the tourist. All I needed after that was the local yellow pages, which I got hold of in the post office on the next street. There was a telephone too – it even worked – and on the eighth try I located the doctor's surgery where Annie had left Katy.

Several possible routes between where I was standing and where I was going presented themselves and I wound my way up and back and up again along three before, on the fourth street, I found a small newsagent's which, unlike the two other shops, three snack bars and one restaurant I'd passed, had no sign in the window banning campers. I picked a copy of the local paper off the pavement rack and went in.

It was empty of customers and the man behind the counter, an Asian of maybe thirty or thirty-five, looked up from a magazine and stubbed out his cigarette as I shut the door behind me and walked towards him. When he asked if he could help me his accent told me he'd grown up in India or Pakistan with English as his second language.

Mine told him I'd grown up in America and after he'd enquired whether I was connected with the American base and I'd said no and paid for the paper, I handed him the photo of Katy I'd been given by her grandmother. He recognised her, that was obvious from the way he smiled.

'Last Monday I believe she came in with a woman who wasn't her mother,' I said.

'Ah,' he said, the smile of recognition widening. He gestured to his hair and made chopped motions with his hands. 'Her nurse friend.'

I was doing well here and hated to dampen his good humour, but I had to tell him the nurse friend was dead. 'You must be one of the last people who saw her before she disappeared. I need to know everything she said to you when she came in here with the girl.'

'But she didn't come in with the girl,' he said. 'She stayed outside. The girl came in on her own.'

'I see . . . would you know if she spoke with anyone outside?'

He thought about this. 'I heard no talking,' he said, 'but I cannot be sure.' He squinted through the racks of magazines and out the shop window towards the street beyond.

'I tell you,' he said finally, 'she was not normal that time. Usually she is very friendly to me and to my wife, who works here sometimes also. She comes in, she asks after our babies. When she did not come in, I looked out. She was like this –' He picked up a paper and held it out in front of himself, unfolded; he looked away into the distance over it with an absent unseeing expression. 'I thought, what is happening out there? That is what it looked like to me – that something must be happening – a fire or a fight, something like that. I went over to the door –' He came out from behind the counter, walked past me towards it, pulled it open – 'and stared out that way too. I saw nothing.'

'It was empty?'

'No. no. Like now.'

The pavements on both sides of the street were crowded with people pushing kids in buggies or carrying shopping bags or rushing with briefcases or talking earnestly. A green American army jeep with half a dozen khaki soldiers in it drove past.

'The little girl pulled at her hand,' he went on, 'and she remembered the earth, you know what I mean? She got out her purse and gave the child money for the sweets and the child came and paid me. The woman smiled and waved to me.' He shook his head. 'But she had not returned. That was very very clear.'

'Oh? How's that?'

He folded the paper and put it under his arm, then turned around and mimed walking away. 'She forgot to pay me for the paper.'

'Did you go after her?'

He shrugged and spread his palms out before him. 'Why? I knew she would be in again.'

Claudine looked up when I came in and said, 'No luck, eh?'

I dropped into the chair by her desk and told her what I'd found out. 'Only the police have the resources to track down everyone who was on the street when Annie Murphy was, but they're too convinced of their circumstantial case against Gillian to see why they should.'

'You asked them?'

'As I was there, I thought I might as well.'

'And the receptionist at the doctor's surgery?'

I pointed my thumb at the floor. 'Anything exciting happen here while I was out?'

'Only the thing on the news about Nicola.'

'Oh? What thing was that?'

She looked a little surprised. 'About her defending that woman they arrested up in Manchester, the one they say makes bombs for the IRA.'

A red net dropped from nowhere over my mind, raising my emotional temperature so sharply it made me stand up. 'Is Suze in?' I demanded.

She sat back, out of the blast area, and nodded. 'She walked in just before you did.'

I proceeded into my office and straight across to the interconnecting door, which I tapped with my knuckle and opened without pausing. Suze looked up from the brief she was reading and grinned. Her coat was still on and she hadn't even sat down yet. 'Cuppa?' she offered, dropping the brief on her desk.

'Sure.'

She rubbed her hands and walked towards the sideboard.

'God,' she said, 'isn't it freezing out there? Do you know they still haven't fixed that damn heating unit in Court 3 at Marylebone? It's been broken since before Christmas. Everybody sits there with their coats on. It's outrageous.'

'Mmmm, absolutely,' I mumbled, watching as she checked the water level in the electric kettle and pressed it on. But my disgruntlement was too impatient to abide chat. I walked in as far as her desk and propped one thigh over the corner of it, registering but not caring about the splashes of mud on my leather boots and the hems of my black wool trousers. 'Suze,' I said, 'I'm unhappy about this IRA case Nicola's accepted. It's controversial and we agreed a long time ago that controversial cases need approval from both of us. At the very least I'd have appreciated being told about it before it was on the news.'

She'd turned on the ascot, which exploded with an unhealthy bang, and was rinsing the mugs. Over her shoulder she said, 'Actually I only knew a few minutes beforehand myself.'

'Are you kidding? She didn't even get *your* approval?'

'She was excited,' she said without turning around. She began to dry one of the mugs. 'Someone in Manchester put her name forward and she drove straight up there last night.'

My thigh slid off the desk and I walked over to her. 'She could have consulted us *twelve hours ago?*'

Now she did turn. Her jaw had tightened and her tone gave an early warning of impatience. 'For Christ's sake, Dee, the client's pleading not guilty.'

'I should hope so.'

The impatience burst out. 'Don't be so narrow minded,' she said, waving the cup at me. 'In case you haven't noticed they've been rounding up alleged IRA suspects right and left the past few days. Something big is brewing and it'll be good for us to be involved.'

I rolled my eyes at the ceiling. 'I'm not going to have another argument with you about publicity. That's not the point.'

'No, the point is that you just don't *like* Nicola Steyning.'

'Like doesn't enter into it. I don't trust her. I simply cannot believe she's abandoned her political ambitions. I think she's here because we'll look good on her CV.'

She thumped the mug on the sideboard. 'Since *when* are you against political ambition? Aren't you forgetting that I met her because of my *own* political work?'

'Oh God, I wasn't insulting you . . .'

'I think that's for me to determine. *I* brought Nicola Steyning into this firm.'

'I'm all too aware of that. What I can't pretend is that it imbues her with some kind of immaculate dispensation. I think we should take it to the Monday morning meeting – see what the associates have to say. It's their reputation too.'

At that she nodded a single abrupt nod and turned her back on me again. I left without the cup of tea.

Black thoughts pushed me right up to the precipice of despond: *I'd made a mistake staying with the firm – I should have moved north with David – this pregnancy was a message, even if I wasn't sure from whom.* Then a telephone call cut across them, pulling me back. Mary Mackay, the pathologist I'd hired, had done her usual quick work.

'I'd have been back to you even faster if I hadn't met so much obstruction this morning,' she said after I tried to thank her.

'Don't tell me Moleham police didn't want to co-operate . . .'

'I wasn't going to. I had a fax copy of their pathologist's report an hour after I asked for it. It was the Home Office that erected the barricades.'

Fortunately she'd taught a number of now senior Home Office doctors many of the things they knew and still had a few strings, one of which she'd pulled. When she'd read the result, she decided their caginess must have been a product of embarrassment.

'I've seen some pretty pathetic autopsy reports from that department in my day, God knows,' she said, 'but this tops them all.' Assigned to determine the time of death, they'd measured the relative emptiness of the stomach without bothering to note the trace of barbiturate that she'd found both there and in the blood. Even worse in her view, they'd been satisfied to confirm by eye alone the Moleham pathologist's conclusion that Annie Murphy had died of a broken neck incurred as a result of a fall.

'They're not wrong about that, surely?'

'As it happens they're not, but there *is* a lot of scar on the body – all over the torso and the upper arms and legs: she must have been in a horrific fire when she was five or six years old – and scar tissue is tricky to read even when you're trying. The clotting beneath it is in the correct spots, certainly, for a fall; what I question is whether she was standing on a stool the height of the one at the scene when it happened. I checked for bone fractures – it seemed to me there were too many for the accident described – and I wasn't happy with the result, so I also checked to see if she had particularly brittle bones. She didn't.'

I thought about this a moment. 'What are you saying?' I asked her.

'What I'm saying is that I'm going to do more tests before I make any firm statements, but my working hypothesis is that this woman may have fallen somewhere else and been moved into the situation in which you found her.'

It was as if someone had bumped into me while I'd been holding one of those cardboard kaleidoscope tubes up to the light: all the coloured pebbles rippled and shifted into an entirely different pattern. And I was still staring into it, mulling over its meaning, when George telephoned from Moleham to report in.

'Two items so far. One, it isn't only the woman next door who saw Gillian run from the house: two others in flats opposite also just happened by the miracle of coincidence to be peeping out their net curtains.'

'And to have clocks at their elbows?'

'You got it. The other thing is, those girls are outnumbered on that street – everyone else seems to belong to this right-wing pressure group called MUCK or MALT or . . .'

'MOPE – Moleham Opponents of the Peace Encampment. Don't tell me. At least one of them has attended every camp-related court case I've ever been involved with. Want to hear my news?' I repeated Mary Mackay's opinion.

George, well-known lover of conspiracy theories that he is, was cheered and stimulated, but his instinct was to dismiss the idea that local MOPErs might have organised a cover up, never mind a killing. 'We're talking about a group of very straight, very conventional people between the ages of fifty-five and seventy-five,' he reminded me, 'most of them not terribly fit.'

'You don't need to be fit yourself. You just need to know someone who is.'

'Mmmm, maybe. I still think it's a long shot, but if you want, I'll see what I can root out about a few backgrounds when I go back tomorrow.'

'You're staying over? Why bother? I'd much rather have the information about Tonio Shiraz – he's the person with the most to gain out of this and I could easily imagine him organising it.'

'My new associate's on his case even as we speak, never fear.'

'You have a new associate?'

'Well, she's a freelance – got one of those government enterprise allowances to start her own business. History graduate from one of the polys. Very keen on research. The reason I'm staying over is because it's in your client's interest. I tracked down Annie Murphy's landlord – the police have apparently taken away what they need from her room; he's letting me clear out the rest. She owed a month's rent – I've put it on expenses, along with your contribution towards redecorating. I'll come in tomorrow as early as I can with what I find. Anything else your end?'

'Not really,' I said, giving him, for the record, a short account of my conversation with little Katy, my efforts to reach him after I'd seen her and my own disappointing trip to Moleham. 'The only thing the newsagent remembered noticing about Annie Murphy was her absent-mindedness.'

'Absent-mindedness?'

'She picked a newspaper off the rack on the pavement . . .' I started.

Then I heard what I'd said.

The newsagent in Moleham, like others in the trade, not only opened early in the morning, he knew the reading habits of his regulars: Annie Murphy's paper had been The *Guardian*. She hadn't had it opened out to a double spread, he was quite positive about this; she'd been glancing over either the front page or the back.

By eight thirty I'd collected a copy of the ten-day-old edition from the paper's editorial offices; by nine fifteen I was back in the waiting room at Holloway Prison. When they let me see Gillian twenty minutes later, I had distilled my questions.

This time she was almost herself: the sedated dullness had gone and her springy hair was frizzing out around her head again as usual. After a quick 'Hi' and a wave, and before she'd even sat down, she asked 'How's Katy?' I described in minutest detail my visit with her daughter, repeated it all again under questioning, then reported the results so far of the investigations going on in her name.

As I was talking I could see the intensity in her expression relaxing, and when I finished she leaned across the table and said 'Is there a chance of bail?'

'I haven't got quite enough evidence to make an application, but we're getting there. You only get one shot at it – you know that? – so I want to be sure we win it. Meanwhile I'm looking into the idea that Annie went off abruptly like she did because of something she read in the paper. Maybe something was going on in her personal life that was connected . . .'

'Yes – well – she was one of those people who can talk a lot without telling you much about themselves, you know?'

'Do you mind if I quiz you anyway?'

She slouched down into her chair and pulled the misshapen black cardigan across her front. 'No. Of course not. Anything if it gets me out of here quicker.'

I started with the most likely news story, a small item on the bottom of the back page about new medical proof of the old allegation that the American military authorities at Moleham and the other nuclear bases in Britain were bombarding the peace camps outside their fences with ultra low-frequency sound waves. Common symptoms were nausea, headaches, deafness, memory loss – and paranoia.

'Thank goodness too,' Gillian smiled; but then, in a lower, more serious tone she added, 'Actually, Annie was involved in collecting that evidence. The doctor who put it together is based at Moleham General Hospital, which is where Annie did her nurses' training *and* worked as a ward sister. After she left last year to spend more time at the camp she still did the odd bit of temp work there.'

'What's this doctor's name, any idea?'

She frowned while she thought a moment, then shook her head.

'Do you know what Annie's involvement was exactly?'

She glanced over her shoulder at the guard, then leaned towards me slightly. 'She broke into the base a couple of times looking for the source.'

I bent as well. '*Alone?*'

She shook her head. 'A few of them went. I think Lucy – the tall thin Lucy from Chippenham, do you know the one I mean? – I think she was there, but they were very hush hush about it all. Most of the expeditions inside, the idea is to get caught, get publicity, make people realise how unprotected those weapons are and how easy it is to get through to them. These weren't like that. They took advantage of the easy entry the way we kept warning that a terrorist group could do.'

'And did they find the devices that put out these waves?'

She stared through me for a moment or two, then refocused. 'It is quite possible. She never said so but it is certainly possible.'

The next story was about the probable closure of a car factory outside Liverpool and the one after that about a young unemployed Yorkshire miner who'd been killed in an accident. 'Do you know where Annie was from?' I asked.

She thought again. 'I know she went to school in Scotland – somewhere in the southwest I think.'

'She didn't have a Scots accent though, did she?'

'It wasn't a state school, it was a Catholic boarding school. The nuns were Irish.'

'Mmmm, well, with a name like Murphy she must have been some per cent Irish herself – and as it happens two of the stories have an Irish angle. One is about the Anglo-Irish Agreement . . .'

She looked blank.

For thoroughness' sake I read out the names of the Ulster politicians quoted and of the government junior minister dealing with them. When her expression didn't alter I said, 'The other piece is about the IRA – Special Branch had just arrested a suspected leader named Gerard Ryan.'

She rolled her eyes and grunted.

I moved on to the foreign stories, the latest reports from South

Africa, Libya, Beirut, Moscow, but her response didn't improve.

'What about animal liberation?'

'Not her style.'

'Did she follow cricket?'

'Are you kidding?'

'OK, last one: there was a huge drugs bust out in . . .'

'You mean hard drugs? Coke? Heroin?'

'No, just hashish.'

'She didn't smoke *any*thing – she even moved out of range if other people lit up.'

'Yes, well, if I'd been badly burned in a fire I'd probably react that way too.'

She gave me a puzzled look. 'Fire?'

'Did you never see her scars? The pathologist says they're all over her torso, from her neck to her knees and down her arms to her elbows. She's been like that apparently since she was five or six – I'm working on the theory that this was when her parents died and I was hoping she might have said something to you.'

But Gillian had started to laugh and shake her head and couldn't seem to stop. The guard was looking at me, half enquiring what was up, half about to come over and see for herself, so I reached out and gripped Gillian's hand and spoke her name as a reprimand.

Abruptly she regained control. 'I don't believe it,' she said. 'She went to such lengths to change in the bathroom when I was around – I thought it was *me*. I thought she was nervous I might come on to her.' Then she covered her face with her hands.

Besides looking outwards from Annie's life for a connection to the news, I wanted to start with the news and look behind the stories for a sign of Annie. The investigative journalist I trusted most, Vic Phillips, would undoubtedly help me out if I asked him, but as he'd just returned to work after two weeks' paternity leave, I couldn't imagine him getting around to anything not directly related to a hot story for a while yet. George and his new research associate would work a lot faster, especially if I could tell them exactly what I needed, but they had fewer of the right contacts than Vic.

When I met Theresa O'Connor at Tottenham Court Road Station and we headed down Charing Cross Road towards Soho for the lunch rescheduled from the day before, I was still undecided about which way to step next.

'How's the big case?' I asked her when the greetings were out of the way.

Her melodramatic grunt said, Don't ask, but she stopped and twirled like a model, heedless of the hostile looks of the displaced passers-by cutting around her. She said, 'You see before you Gerard Ryan's ex-solicitor.'

I stopped too, equally heedless. 'What happened?'

She shrugged and resumed walking. 'We had two highly constructive meetings and then I received a message to say my services would no longer be required. When I went over to Brixton to ask him what the hell was going on, I found out he'd been moved – they're not saying where. I thought it was me – no, seriously, you know how I am – but no other solicitor's been hired as far as I can tell and now I've been retained by two of the other IRA suspects they've arrested.' She slowed and when I did the same she bent towards me and whispered, 'They were both picked up the evening Ryan gave me the sack and went to ground.' She straightened and raised her brows at me.

I cleaned an ear with my index finger. 'Excuse me?'

She pushed her red glasses frames back up the bridge of her nose, down which they had slid. 'You heard me,' she said.

It was only as we were standing at the counter waiting to pay our bill an hour later that I realised she'd given me a certain impression which I needed to double check. 'You haven't tipped the press?' I said.

She waved a hand dismissively. '*Invite* disruption of my peace and quiet? You must be joking.'

When I explained my problem, however, and told her what I wanted to do about it, she volunteered to martyr herself for my sake.

Vic Phillips, hearing the magic word 'tip', agreed to meet me at a new pub near Chalk Farm on his way home and when I arrived a little after six, he was sitting by a table at the back, a half-empty pint glass of something no doubt pure and real at his elbow, apparently reading. In fact he was looking at photos – so I saw as he glanced up and flashed me one of his endearing 'trust me' grins. He shows a lot of perfect white tooth when he does this and even though he hides his round spaniel eyes behind large and even rounder tortoise-shell glasses, they're always the first thing I see and they always make me want to pat him on the head. Today I gave in.

He leaned up and gave me a kiss on the cheek. 'Look,' he said, handing me a pile of baby pictures. I took them out of politeness (*baby pictures – just what I needed*), shuffled them quickly and handed them back. I had to be careful; new parent bliss is notoriously contagious.

'So –' he said as he closed the paper wallet and slipped it into the briefcase on the seat beside him. 'Someone's just told me the Home Office is threatening to crack down on Indian children adopted out in India and brought here without prior clearance. It sounded like you.'

'It's the firm,' I nodded.

He waited and when I said no more, he said, 'I've also heard there's a case coming up that could force local authorities to provide water and rubbish collection services to peace camps.' He raised his right eyebrow.

'Jones Davies Cusack are handling that. Tina Cusack.' I smiled at him. 'Give up?'

He started to shrug, but instead tried one more guess: 'It's not a certain radical barrister's indiscretions with a certain lady from another chambers at a recent international conference?'

'Who was *that*?'

But he waved my curiosity aside. 'You're the one who's meant to be doing the talking,' he smiled.

I told him about Annie's death and the charges against Gillian, then described the approach I was taking to the defence and, pretending not to notice the scepticism that had come over his expression, handed him my list of potted news stories.

As he scanned the page, I watched him trying not to smirk. 'I see,' he said, scratching his chin through his day's growth. 'So you want me to find out whether this dead woman was some kind of Libyan-trained animal liberationist who imported Lebanese hash, idolised Ian Botham, had a brother who's a cop, a brother who's in the peace convoy and a brother who's a miner up in Yorkshire.' He lowered the list. 'Don't you want me to check that she wasn't a member of the African National Congress? Or how about the Provos? or . . .'

'Smart ass,' I said, whipping the page out of his hands. 'I'll have you know I have already dealt with the IRA angle this very afternoon. In fact the little tip I had it in mind to – how shall I put it? – "offer in exchange for your assistance in this particular matter" related to that very subject. But –' I shrugged and made out that I was putting the page back into my briefcase.

He reached out and stopped my hand. No longer was he toothsome. 'What?' he said.

'You know this senior IRA man Gerard Ryan, the one they say is . . .'

'. . . I know who he is. Someone told me he'd hired Theresa.'

'Yes, well, he sacked her and was moved out of Brixton – the same day all those other IRA suspects were arrested.'

Every last bit of humour was now completely gone from Vic's expression and he was frowning at me so intently that his eyebrows joined into one. 'Gerard Ryan?' he murmured. He took a swig of his drink and carried on, still more to himself than to me. 'He's the last person I'd have imagined . . . There's never been an IRA supergrass trial in London before, do you realise that? My God, I wonder how soon *that* will be.'

'I'm sure your sources will know more about that than mine.' I unfolded my piece of paper again. 'Speaking of which . . .'

He stared at my hands. Then he took the paper from me and re-examined it, this time without the smirk. 'I'm due for a chat in the next day or two with a certain small animal known for tunnelling around in the dirt. I'll have a word with him about this American air force story and these ones about the Middle East. I'll get one of the juniors to chase the others.'

'Thanks,' I nodded. 'Whatever you can dig up.' Then, because I couldn't resist: 'This wouldn't by any chance be the same "small animal" *The Sun* claims is "using" a certain left-wing journalist?'

He didn't see the joke at all. 'Don't you start on me too, Dee. Do you know there are people who won't speak to me now because of that damned rumour?'

I laughed.

'No really,' he protested. 'I was just setting up to look into the old story about how MI5 "disappears" people from time to time down some bottomless pit in the countryside and my first two interviews both cancelled out on me.' He knocked back the last swallow of his beer. 'I tell you, if I had the money to pay you for a libel action . . .'

'I think it might take more than money honey,' I said, trying to chivvy him back to good humour. 'A mole inside the security services is hardly going to come forward to back you up. And how do you know you're *not* being used?'

'The same way *you* decide whether your clients are innocent.' He patted his stomach. 'You trust what's in here.'

Three

The bruises and scratches don't hurt and the wrung-out rag feeling, I decide, is muscular and can be overcome.

I begin with my legs and, lifting them enough to kick off the blanket, do a laborious series of bends and extensions. I switch to my arms – my neck and head – my wrists – my ankles.

Finally I feel ready and by pushing get the soles of my feet to the floor and my torso balanced over my pelvis. I steady myself and take a step, steady myself, take another step. My body is working but the fit's wrong – like that time in school when I put on someone else's jacket by mistake: I miss all the old bus tickets and gum wrappers in the pocket but can't quite figure out why.

Suddenly a human wail starts up somewhere behind me – lifts an octave – penetrates the top pocket of mind where no sound is supposed to intrude. My heart begins to bang against my chest – *it's a woman, she's being attacked.* The floor starts to tilt. As I stumble forward, one of my hands lands on fabric, which I grab to brace myself. Miraculously I don't fall over and the wooziness eventually subsides. When it does I realise that the wail has decelerated into a bawl and that its source is an unhappy baby.

What I'm clutching turns out to be a curtain and when I comprehend this I draw its side edge back half an inch and stare out the window into the night. I am at least three storeys up, overlooking a narrow road which is deserted beneath the chemical yellow light of a single street lamp several hundred yards to the right. Across the way is the shell of a concrete building, derelict and burned out, large enough to have been a school, perhaps, or maybe a hotel. Bordering it to either side are stretches of corrugated hoarding covered in indecipherable posters and crumbling down from the pressure of the tree root growth on the other side.

To the left I see in silhouette a trio of distant tower blocks and as I watch, blinking red lights pass over them, turn, and pass back the other way. I hear far away the sound of a motor and am deciding that the two things add up to a circling helicopter when a new noise, a roaring, begins behind me, initially reminding me of the childhood sound of my father blowing his lips in my ear. As it gets louder and louder and then even louder still, I feel increasingly certain that if it is a low-flying plane it's going to crash right into this room. I hug my arms over my head and am on the point of crouching down when just at the crash point the noise changes. It's not above, it's out in the street. It's a swarm of hotrod cars zooming past like so many angry bees.

Abruptly all goes quiet, and after a long stretch of stillness I decide it must be OK to let my ears out again. As I lower my hands a dog starts howling somewhere in the distance and when it finishes another takes up. For about five minutes they engage in call and response: yip yip yip yip, woof woof woof woof, yip yip yip yip, back and forth.

Perhaps the dawn is not far away now.

I look out once more and, as I do, white high-beams cut slices of illumination in the darkness to my left. A jeep comes into view and drives past, trailed first by one small rumbling tank, then by another. Leaning out of the top of each of them is a single soldier in jungle camouflage uniform and beret, pointing a machine gun into the emptiness.

Now I do crouch down.

Has London been invaded?

No – that's mad. This isn't London.

Surely not.

I close my eyes, think hard. These aren't the first tanks I've seen recently. Where were the others? Moleham? The TV? A film?

Then I remember.

1

It was early afternoon – Friday afternoon – a week after Claudine and I had found Annie Murphy's body, five days since Gillian's arrest. Not only did I feel I was getting no closer to whoever it was who knew the truth about the death and where it had taken place, I'd had to waste the better part of the day in court on another almost equally frustrating case. Worse still, the now customary nausea hadn't lifted in late morning.

I thought: if Suze is in, I'll apologise for the other day – tell her what's happened – see what she thinks about it.

But Suze was coming out of her office with her coat half on as I pushed open the internal door and when the couple in the reception area stood up and put out their hands to her, I knew I'd missed my chance. She grinned when she saw me, the other day forgotten, and rippled her gloved fingers in a wave; I thought I returned the greeting before stooping to pull off my muddy boots, but as she was passing, she paused and peered into my face. 'Everything OK?' she asked me.

I nodded. What else could I do? I said, 'You coming back this afternoon?'

She shook her head. 'I'm at Elephant and Castle till five-ish and I've got to be at a police committee meeting at 5.30. Mum's down at Tom's' – Tom was her brother – 'so I'm going there for dinner. Tomorrow I'm taking her out and about.' She wrinkled her nose. 'Want to have a meal Sunday night?'

I heard myself tell her that I might be going away (going away? Where the hell was I going?) but promised to give her a call if I didn't.

I started off in search of my colleague Simone, forgetting for that moment the pregnant woman she was now, remembering only the colleague and friend who could always make you feel you had her full attention. Luckily she'd just gone out. So had Maggie. Rita was in, but when I peeked through the window in her door the first thing I saw was the mounted photo of her turbaned husband and their three school-age children on the wall behind her head. I waved at her and passed on. Nicola was in too – I could hear that laugh of hers – and the sound provoked such an unreasoning lump of dark emotion that I abandoned my quest for a sympathetic shoulder and pushed open the door to my office.

Claudine looked across at me between heavy lids and puffy sinuses and sniffed a slushy snuffle. 'George Abbulbee's jusd levd. He broughd in sumb boxes. He – oh – ah – scuse'be –' she fumbled with a balled-up tissue and got it to her nose just in time to catch a series of short quick sneezes. At the end of it she sniffed again and said, 'He'll be back in a quarter of an hour or so.' Then she slid the messages spike towards me and I pulled off the one that was impaled on it. 'The pathologist's assistant rang,' she'd written. 'The pathologist's gone down with flu but wanted you to know that she's finished testing the angle of Annie Murphy's fall and is now 90 per cent certain that her neck was broken by a much longer, steeper drop. She's hoping to fill in more detail with more tests and will get back to you as soon as.'

I smiled at her. 'I needed that. You've made my day.' Then I pointed to the door. 'Now go home.'

Her hand swept across the dictaphone and files. 'But . . .'

'No buts,' I said, imposing my authority. And as limp a thing as that seemed to me, she bowed to it.

I took it for granted without even really considering it that I would wait until George came back before I looked in the boxes he'd left in my office; he'd set them down, though, just beneath the ailing begonia I checked on whenever I came in and as I was doing that my eye was caught and pulled down by something royal blue. The top box in the stack was open and this royal blue something sticking out of it was wrapped in clear plastic and seemed to have the surface texture of chenille. Before I could stop it my hand was reaching in: was it knitting, I wondered, or crochet? Or was it maybe weaving?

I lifted it out in order to decide, a long piece that close-up was obviously hand knitting, probably the back of a sweater. Figured into it using three other shades of blue, a little red, a little yellow and some black was an intricate pattern of some kind.

I held it out at arm's length. The shape was a Celtic knot.
Exquisite.

I laid it over the back of the chair and looked to see what had been under it in the box. What I found was clothes: nurses' uniforms, sweaters, jeans, T-shirts, a couple of skirts, a couple of jackets, all of them pretty well worn, all of them a size 8. When I got through them and through the layer of shoes and boots and slippers to the blank flat cardboard bottom, I felt – I don't know – almost annoyed at her, almost peeved that she'd gone and died without explaining herself to me.

Dee, Dee, oh Dee, I thought, did you expect she'd pop out of the box like Jack? Did you imagine her few belongings might speak to you? Did you believe you could unpack the truth of her?

I turned to the second box, which contained a jumble of books, papers and loose prints, including the obligatory strip of goofy shots snapped in a picture booth somewhere. George had obviously emptied a drawer by scooping up the contents between his hands and dumping them in from a height. I didn't just at that moment fancy the task of sorting through them any more than he had (*An – nie where a r e you?*) but out of duty I reached in at random.

My hand landed on a soft object, rectangular, fairly heavy, which proved to be a cushioned box covered in purple satin, now worn at the corner and stained with time. The broken lock on the front of it made me think of the box where I'd hidden my secret diary as a girl and the memory made me prise the halves apart with a mixture of trepidation and anticipation. There was no secret diary here though, only two strings of rosary beads – one flecked with hardened red paint, the other a child's – plus a Kodak snapshot dated 1970 showing a woman pushing a buggy full of shopping with a little girl walking at her side, and a volume of Catholic catechism that smelled as if it had been sprayed by a tom. Inside its front cover was a stamp saying 'Property of St Mary Magdalene Catholic School for Girls, Dalabbey Village, Dumfries'.

I dipped into the cardboard box again and this time pulled out a paperback novel with a vaguely familiar title which a cover quote called 'The controversial bestseller they tried to suppress'. I turned it over to read the blurb and it came back to me why I'd heard about it: it was that American one from the early seventies about a physics student who figures out the recipe for a nuclear bomb using declassified information.

On my third try my fingers came to rest on a paper wallet, I presumed full of photographs, and as I lifted it out, one of them escaped and spiralled to the floor. It turned out to be a peace movement postcard captioned 'This scepter'd isle' and showing a map of Britain with yellow dots all over it marking out the spots where the major American military bases are located. Annie (or someone) had ringed five of these, including Moleham, with red ink.

I was about to go through the wallet when George walked in, called out hello, and, waving at me to stay put, headed straight for the radiator at the back of the room where he stood for a moment lathering his hands over the heat. He looked different and after a moment I realised why: he'd at long last given up combing those strands of hair across his pate. He'd come out as a bald man.

'It suits you,' I said, patting the top of my head.

His shrug was dismissive. 'It's wind and waterproof.'

'You discovered this or you were persuaded?'

He moved over to the sideboard and felt the side of the jug sitting on the hotplate of the percolator. 'It's Lou's fault.'

'Lou?'

'Louise, my new assistant. Is this stuff drinkable?'

'Compared to what you're used to? Yes.'

He helped himself, sipped without so much as a cringe, then propped himself on the arm of the chair in front of my desk. He hadn't taken off his duffle coat and when he'd set the cup down, fished in his pockets and withdrew a notebook.

He opened to a middle page and ran through what he'd found out so far about Tonio Shiraz: first, the statement he'd given the police said he'd been on the motorway heading for an appointment in Nottingham at the time of Annie's death; second, he'd since produced the log for his car phone, which seemed to support his claim that he'd talked to his office several times and to various clients but not to his ex-wife; third, the customer in Nottingham had vouched for his arrival time; fourth, the police hadn't seen any need to press him for his whereabouts later that day. They also hadn't seemed bothered by what George considered a suspiciously coincidental gap in Telecom's records: their information was that the phone on Annie's landing had been out of order at the time Gillian claimed she'd been shouting down it at Tonio; what further explanation was needed?

'You reckon British Telecom files can be fiddled?'

'Come on, anything can be fiddled if you know the right people.'

'And he knows them?'

'This is what I want to find out next. I also want to look into her movements a bit more.' He held up a photo of a dark woman with thick black hair, large eyes and a wide mouth full of white teeth. 'The new Mrs Shiraz,' he said. 'According to previous neighbours she was diagnosed infertile during her first marriage and hasn't come to terms with this. She's desperate for a kid.'

'Yes, well, in that case getting rid of Gillian would have been more use to her than getting rid of Annie.'

'It's a stone, that's all I'm saying; it ought to be properly turned over. I'm scratching around Shiraz anyway; I might as well scratch around her some more while I'm at it.'

I shrugged at that and said sure, why not. Then I asked how he'd fared during his second go-round with the local band of high-minded citizenry.

He leaned towards me, grinning. 'At 8 p.m. the night Annie died, *every single one* of her immediate neighbours was visited by two members of a party of Jehovah's Witnesses.'

He sat back looking expectant, as if awaiting a sign that I'd heard a trumpet fanfare, but it didn't sound for me. When he perceived this, he shook his head as if to say, 'You disappoint me, Dee old girl' and took a bunch of polaroids out of his top left jacket pocket. They were dark night-time shots, apparently of the back of a row of houses, and at first I didn't see the relevance of these either. Then I recognised the stairs: it was the rear of Annie's place.

'Whoever's behind this knows what they're doing,' he said. 'They made sure everyone who was around was distracted, then brought the body in through the back door. Leaving the window open was undoubtedly intentional, to make certain the decomposition process was as slow as possible. They wanted whoever found the body to do exactly what you did: assume the death was more recent than it was; not ask questions.'

'What about the Jehovah's Witnesses? Do you think they had any idea . . .?'

'Their area organiser was rung up and *invited* to send a group of missionaries. They're pacifists, you know; they enjoy the challenge of bringing the word to the pro-militarists.'

'Yes, I've heard that. Rung up by whom?'

'A "Mr Smith".' He smiled.

I frowned. 'And you think this "Smith" then hung around idly waiting for them to arrive?'

'He didn't need to. The Jehovah's Witnesses work to schedules. He knew when they would be there, give or take twenty minutes.'

I still wasn't sure but said, 'You'll keep on this?'

He nodded 'of course.'

'How about the fire that killed her family – any inspirations on how we trace *that*?'

'I can trawl the death registers for the southwest Scottish region within a radius of that convent school where she boarded – look up all the Murphys who died in the period – but that assumes she was raised around there, which may or may not be true. I'd much rather pursue other strands.'

'I've got one or two myself . . .' I started, reaching for my notes. But as I was doing this he got up and crossed to the stack of boxes, where he knelt and fumbled around first in one of them, then in the next, then in a third.

'Ah ha!' he said at last over his shoulder. He withdrew a folder, opened it as he stood up again, came to my desk and dropped a narrow sheet of contact prints in front of me. 'This strand for instance.'

I held it up to the light. The top strip showed a jeep – several jeeps clustered together – a coach painted with camouflage foliage – a tank – two tanks – soldiers at a shooting range – soldiers in formation, rifles against shoulders. The middle one showed guard towers with search-lights pointing towards the ground – fence work – a gate – a woods area. The third showed – front-on, side-on and from above – an enormous flat-bed truck with huge long silver things on it. I brought the sheet closer to my eyes and squinted at this last. There was writing on the sides of the silver things: United States of America.

I suddenly realised what they were.

'Jeez,' I murmured.

George said, 'It wasn't hidden. If it was sinister I'd have expected to find it in the mattress or under the rug or somewhere like that. On the other hand...'

'On the other hand she did make at least two surreptitious forays into Moleham Air Base.'

'Did she now. Who told you this?'

'Gillian. It struck me that Annie might have gone off because of something in the paper she was reading before she vanished. I looked it up and lo and behold a doctor in Moleham had just published research which supported the old claim that the American military have been bombarding the peace camps beside their nuclear bases with ultra low-frequency sound waves, making everybody ill. According to Gillian, Annie was in the group looking for the source of the waves at Moleham.'

'I'll find this doctor and talk to him,' he said. 'Anything else?'

I glanced down at my notes and saw the two other little points I'd intended asking him to investigate. I heard myself say, 'No, that's enough. I'll handle the rest myself over the weekend.'

When he'd gone, I found myself up on my feet and crossing my small office to the filing cabinet, where involuntarily, it seemed, I knelt, pulled open the deep bottom drawer, reached to the back and, after rooting around, lifted out the newspaper-wrapped parcel that I'd buried there with such finality six weeks before. A small inner voice tried to urge caution on me but I didn't want to hear it. I tore off the paper and looked hard again into that framed and preserved memory of David and me up in Skye. Taken by a lone passing tourist one of the times we'd forced ourselves out of bed to buy food, it showed us standing facing each other on the pier which jutted out into the bay in front of our small hotel. You could see the sun setting behind the snow-capped mountain in the distance and the fire of the clouds reflected in the still surface of the water. We both had on muddy wellies and ancient windbreakers and our hairdos were designed by wind and rain. His arms were around my shoulders, mine were around his waist and he was laughing down at me with an expression that made me feel like an intruder just looking at the photo. I could feel the tears rising and suddenly had to turn the thing face down on my desk.

What's wrong with you, Dee. You know it wasn't like that. The reality – can you have forgotten? – The reality was a guy who didn't pull out of his bad time at the rate or in the way you thought he would, a guy whose retreat into his past seemed to cut you out of his future.

You felt he should have been sorrier to move away.

You felt he didn't make enough gestures to you.

I wrapped the photo back up and stared at the lump it made while the chattering debate went on in my head: on the one hand, on the other, maybe this, maybe that. Then, slowly, deliberately, I put the parcel back in the bottom drawer of the filing cabinet, rolled it closed, locked it up, and walked back across the room to my desk. There I picked the British Rail timetable from the bookshelf and spent some time thinking things through and looking things up. Finally I straightened and reached for the telephone.

II

Once I'd established that the Mother Superior who'd presided over the St Mary Magdalene Convent School in Annie Murphy's day was, *mirabile dictu* (as she put it) still there and free to see me the following afternoon, it was common sense that I should break my journey up to Dumfries with a visit to the family of the young unemployed miner whose death had been in the news the day Annie disappeared. Asking Pegs Millar to set up that visit seemed equally logical; after all, she *was* active in the Women Against Pit Closures group in the same region of south Yorkshire. And when she not only said of course she'd do it but invited me to spend the night, there wasn't so much as a hint in my surprised response that the duck had come down.

It was only after the dead man's sister picked me up at the station the next afternoon and we set off at about ten miles an hour into a swirling white curtain of horizontal snow that the truth began to ooze out from beneath the blanket of virtuous excuses I'd thrown over it: I could have spoken to her on the telephone. I needn't have dragged her from her nice warm fireside to discover what I'd gleaned during snatched conversation as we slipped and slithered back and forth across those invisible country lanes, namely that her brother had been a nice stay-at-home provincial lad likely to have met Annie Murphy only if she'd stopped into his local or sat beside him at a football match. Worse, the hour I spent with the young man's distressed parents and fiancée reinforced this probability.

I contrived to get myself out of there as soon as I could and, thanks to a taxi driver eager to show off his new tyre chains, caught an early train and arrived at the station nearest to the village where Pegs Millar lived two and a half hours before I'd told her to expect me. It was there, standing on the platform watching the train I'd just got off disappear north, that the single small fact which I'd managed to let slip from my mind crawled back into it: this wasn't merely the local station for the village where Pegs lived. It was the local station for the village of another old friend as well: her cousin, Dr David Blake.

I contemplated the steamed-over window of the platform café; I even put my hand on its door. Then I thought: you can't be serious. Here you are, not ten minutes from his house. You have conned people and set them up – set yourself up – to create just this opportunity. And now instead of seizing it you propose to dawdle over a plastic cup full of overstewed tea.

I looked outside. The sun was making the clouds glow from behind as it tried to push its way out. A double-decker bus was sitting at the stop, engine off, queue waiting to board. I joined the end of it just as the driver climbed up into the cab.

Ten minutes later the hydraulic doors hissed open and disgorged me on to the pavement in front of the general store, off-licence and post office that is the prime amenity of Holmsby village. I decided the conversation might be a lot easier if it were lubricated, then succumbed to further silliness and bought a box of those chocolates he likes but only ever eats on special occasions.

When I re-emerged, snow was coming down again, this time in a magic rain of powdery flakes. I forced my feet quicker and quicker along the slushy pavement out of the village until all of a sudden there I was, on the corner of the familiar shaded cul-de-sac, now overhung by ice-coated branches. No one had been by with the salt in a while and half a dozen or so cars, clearly untouched since the snowy weather had settled in, looked like frozen mounds, as one with the ground. I did not see his among them.

I set off on the precarious passage to his front gate, which I reached with all my parts intact. Lights were on in the front rooms, but that didn't necessarily mean anything. David supported the miners by running up huge electricity bills.

I reached out to push the gate, then withdrew my hand, having a serious attack now of second thoughts.

What would he say?

What would I say?

I stepped back, turned, started to retreat to the corner. Ten steps later, I stopped.

This was stupid. I was a grown-up. This was a guy I knew well.

I returned to the gate with renewed determination, grabbed hold of it firmly, pushed it open, walked down the unshovelled path and paused at the foot of the steps. There was a hum, an electrical buzz, coming from inside.

Was I about to catch David Blake on one of his biannual cleaning sprees? What a laugh that would be.

I continued on up the steps to the door.

Yes, it was definitely the noise of vacuuming.

I pushed the bell, which made one of those chime tones that goes 'b i n g   b o n g'. It brought to mind that old commercial – 'b i n g   b o n g, Avon calling' – and the memory amused this fretful, nervous me so much that as I heard the motor cut out and the feet approach, I prepared to go into a silly pose involving the box of chocolates. If I noticed anything at all odd about the weight of the footfall, I must have put it down to the muffling effect of the carpet: I was that keyed up, that tingly with readiness to speak my jokey hello.

The knob turned. My heart was going ka-boomity boom, ka-boomity boom, much too fast.

The door opened.

I grinned up at where six-foot eyes are. Five-foot-seven eyes stared back.

She was blonde (like his late wife); very pretty. Very young.

'Yes?' she smiled. She had lovely teeth. 'May I help you?' She was also very local.

I pretended I'd come to the wrong house. It was how I felt.

Over the next half hour I lived a complete Victorian melodrama. I walked the streets alone. I eyed the railway tracks, the bridges, the edge of the desolate moor with bleak regard. I forgot I was supposed to be a feminist. I cursed David Blake for the umpteenth time for not being the knight I'd yearned for, the soul mate I'd fantasised, the father figure whose shoulder I needed. I reminded myself brutally that I'd known this would happen – *known* he'd go off with one of her type. It had always amazed me – *always* – that he'd stayed with me: I'd felt when I'd let myself think about it like the scruffy kid sister, the one He turns to when She, his tall slender patrician wife, is found dead in bed with another man.

The cold suddenly got through to me again and, pulling myself together, I headed back the way I'd come. I would go home, that's what I would do – go home and start over.

But when I got back to the station, I discovered that the London train had been delayed by the bad weather.

I looked over at the station clock just as the pub doors beneath it opened. I let them draw me in and by the time Pegs found me there, I was feeling a lot better.

'Sorry I'm late,' she apologised in her scratchy timbre. Before I'd met her, when I'd only spoken to her on the phone, that voice had conjured up a blousy bottled blonde, waistless with middle age and kept alive by a diet of bad scotch and cigarettes. Actually (or 'in actual fact', as she would say) she was long and thin – no, not thin, *skinny* – with greying brown hair, and though most of her socialising was done in pubs like this one, the only thing she seemed to have picked up was the skill of making a half last until closing time – that and a dirty laugh. What was accurate was the part about the cigarettes. She was a supplementary benefit smoker: she did it because it was cheaper than eating.

She began searching in her bag while I went to get her usual and was still at it when I set it on the table in front of her. Without looking up she thanked me and said, 'David's working the night shift at the hospital this weekend.'

I felt a rush around my ears, like I get when I look down from a high place, but she didn't appear to hear it.

She found her packet of fags at last and after offering it to me, took one for herself. 'I wasn't sure whether I was meant to tell him you were coming.'

I forced my lips over my teeth in what should have been a smile but may have resembled Dracula's hungry look. I drank and tried adjusting it. A voice floated out of my mouth, squeaky and uneven: 'We made a deal not to speak, you know . . .'

Her right brow arched high with scepticism; her eyes said 'pull the other one'. She leaned sideways towards me and spoke from the corner of her mouth. 'He tried to phone you when he was up in town a couple of weeks ago. I know this for a fact.'

I thought, She can't know about the young blonde.

I turned away, drank again. Then, as I stared into my glass: 'Surely he can't be lacking for female company here. A nice attractive doctor, available . . . they must be queuing up to iron his shirts.'

She was signalling to the bar maid with her empty match box. 'He's not paying any attention if they are,' she smiled over her arm. 'My friend's daughter Rosie, who's available and attractive herself, leapt at the job of cleaning for him once a week, but he looks right through her.'

I glanced up sharply and can only think my mouth was wide open. 'I thought that'd get you going,' she laughed. She pointed to her chest. 'I accept full responsibility. *I* was the one who pushed him into it. His place was an absolute tip.'

I expect I said something to this – I must have, I'm a polite person – before I excused myself, went into the ladies and looked into the mirror. Yes, there was definitely an ass where my face usually sat, but at least it was chuckling at me.

I gave the box of chocolates to Pegs' and Harry's children and we had the wine with supper. I think I drank most of it and my rate didn't slacken much afterwards, when we decamped to their local. I had several intense conversations with several people I'd met on earlier visits, and David's name, so far as I can remember, wasn't mentioned in any of them, yet I started to be aware of a steady pressure on me to mosey on out to the call box and give him a ring at the hospital. No matter how volubly I talked or how loudly I shouted over the music, or how maniacally I threw darts at the board, it pulsed away at me, *phone him up, phone him up, phone him up.* Finally at about ten I wandered out into the hall, ostensibly in search of the toilets, but someone was just dialling and two other people were waiting.

The ladies' room was crowded and noisy, with women in various stages of tipsiness sizing up their flaws in front of the mirrors, but my gaze cut right around them all and found the lone woman engrossed in breast-feeding a tiny baby in the far corner.

No, Dee, I thought, no no no.

I went into one of the empty cubicles, locked the door behind me, let in a sheet of frozen air, pulled down my jeans, sat on the seat, put my head in my hands and let the debate have its way with me.

What, it began, is to be achieved by telling him? Do I want him to make up my mind for me?

If I look straight at the situation – no averting the gaze, no filtering it through pink gauze – don't I have to admit that I already know deep down in the sub-basement of my heart which way the decision will go?

I poked around in myself yet again, the way a tongue goes back to a sensitive tooth, testing for a sign of maternal yearning.

Yes –. Just there –. A flicker. But still nowhere near hot enough or bright enough, still too low a flame, to warm me to the idea of going it on my own. . . Which leads back to the business about me uprooting and leaving the firm and London and my friends and moving up here.

I think: I could say to him, these are my terms, take 'em or leave 'em.

Then I think: No. That is called emotional manipulation.

What is more, it begs a key point: we'd had more than enough opportunity to live together in our time and had never done so.

The obvious moment would have been when he'd sold the flat

he'd shared with his wife, but it hadn't been all that long after her death and too soon, it seemed to me. Instead he'd found a little house behind Church Street market, within walking distance of where I lived, and a routine had come into being: a night at his place, nights on our own, a night at my place. We could have broken out of this at any point if one of us had pushed it – we certainly whinged often enough about the inconvenience we imposed on ourselves – but it was as if – I don't know – as if as early love blindness began to fade and partial sightedness developed, our differences separated themselves out and edged ahead of the similarities. He turned out not to like garlic or onions; he preferred rambling with a tent along ridges in the Peak District to lying on sunny beaches (a pastime which had the added virtue as far as I was concerned of not inducing vertigo); he had a tolerance of dust and dirty dishes and full rubbish bags that I did not share; and though he was a more genuine egalitarian than a lot of self-styled New Men who go around interrupting you and booming at you with great authority to tell you how feminist they are, he did still have a side that believed a man's got to do what a man's got to do. He could be bad tempered in the mornings, too.

On the other hand, he put up with my fits of fury and depression, did not judge me and laughed at my jokes. And in his opinion, *I* was the reason we didn't live together; he said I was too used to having my own place, that I didn't just like retreating to it either, I needed to retreat to it. I told him he was a fine one to talk.

Then had come his rediscovery of the north: what he'd left behind twenty-whatever years before now seemed to him real and attractive; what he'd once been drawn to in London seemed intolerably shallow, propped up by poseurs and careerists.

People like Nicola Steyning.

There was a sudden knock on the cubicle door and a voice called, 'You all right in there?' I called back that I was. Frozen but all right.

I flushed the toilet; pulled my trousers back on; shut the window.

No, I decided, no. This impulsive trip up here, the half formulated notion that I'd tell him and go along with however he responded – if I'd behaved the same way ten or fifteen years ago

I'd have rounded on myself for copping out. The truth was, I was *lucky* he wasn't around: I'd been saved from the impulse to duck my obligation to choose. Because that's what it was: *my* obligation – mine, not his, not ours.

Which wasn't to say he didn't deserve to know what had happened. I would definitely tell him. Before I could do that, though, I had to know in my own mind what it was that I wanted.

The next morning I was woken by a cool, damp sensation on my cheek and, opening my eyes, found myself staring into the pointed face of the youngest child, Lilly, who was feeling me with tiny fingers. When I winked and blew out my lips at her, she shrieked and waddled towards the door, nearly bumping into her five-year-old brother Billie, who was walking through it very carefully and very slowly, balancing a cup on a saucer and staring at his burden with fixed attention. I pushed myself up and swung my legs out of the bedclothes, intending to reach out and take it from him. Then I decided not to wreck it for him and just watched silently as he made his way, one slow, careful step at a time, towards me. When he at long last arrived, he handed over the cup and saucer very solemnly, then shook his hands and grinned, real pleased with himself. I thanked him and told him how impressed I was by his delivery of the cup of tea, which I now tasted and found to be spot-hittingly wonderful.

Somehow I'd escaped a hangover.

Billie lingered, watching me drink so intently that I wondered for a moment if he were expecting more chocolates. I said, 'I'll bring the cup back to the kitchen, you don't have to wait.'

He did a self-conscious twirl to the right, then pushed round on the other foot, so he whirled left. Then he said, 'Cousin David'th in the kitchen' and ran out the door.

I dressed in a kind of panic (*David*), combed my hair, added a touch of eyeliner, looked at myself in the full-length mirror on the back of the door, assembled my nerve (*this is ridiculous*) and headed out.

He was reading the paper and so engrossed in it that I was nearly beside him before he glanced up. He got to his feet so fast he knocked the edge of the table with his thighs and sloshed the tea in his cup into the saucer and over the paper and table. Ignoring this, he took a step my way, his arms almost out, as if he were going to give me one of our old hugs. Mine almost went out from the same habit but were overridden by the panic. I took a half shuffle backwards and looked at the tea and the table.

'Oops,' I said.

He now took in the mess and turned to tend to it, sopping at it with a soggy white paper napkin. I reached to lift the newspaper out of the way and as I did so saw the headline and the 'Exclusive' over it.

'Look,' I said, pointing to it. ' "Supergrass Trial Scheduled for London – by Vic Phillips".' I grinned. 'I tipped him this one and he went out and proved it – in *eighteen hours*.' This was easy; talking about our work was always easy. 'I'm on this case, David, you absolutely wouldn't believe . . .'

He nodded. 'So I gathered from Pegs . . .'

'She phoned you?' When had she done that?

He shook his head. 'I phoned her. The girl who opened the door when you stopped in yesterday – she left a note saying an American woman had come by.' He smiled. 'Don't try to tell me you're surprised. You're the one who always says what a small place this is.' The smile broadened, took over his eyes. 'You look well. How *are* you?'

He looked as always – slightly rumpled, very grey, lean and fit in spite of a fondness for pints of bitter and slices of bread like doorstops spread with jam.

I said, 'Oh – fine' and felt come over me an instinct to blush and go all coy. I couldn't help myself, I looked down, and when I did I realised Lilly and Billie were both staring up at us and that the cat and the dog were rivetted as well. I continued my gaze around towards the door, where Pegs was leaning against the jamb in her nightgown, studying her fingernails. Harry was behind her, dressed but barefoot. He appeared to be examining a spot on the ceiling.

David said, 'Why don't we go for a walk?'

'I've got to be in Dumfries . . .' I started.

'I'll get you to your train, don't worry.'

I said OK sure and fetched my coat.

An occasional dry flake fell as we made our way out of the estate and at first neither of us spoke, just walked; then he began to talk about the clinic and the hospital, telling me anecdotes about the staff teams and the problems with morale and money. I wanted to listen to him – wanted to know his news – but a little speech kept flickering across my mind, cutting back and forth over my concentration. 'David,' it went, 'I have something to tell you.' An alternative version went, 'David, there is something you should know.' Still another began, 'Perhaps you should sit down.'

I didn't want to utter any of them – my thoughts of the night before, still with me, seemed right, sensible – but I could feel the pressure (of emotion and tradition and ritual) rising up against the back of my tongue, pushing on my palate.

My mouth was opening – I couldn't seem to hold it closed. I even cleared my throat; then I caught a fragment of the sense of what David was saying.

'What?' I said. Or perhaps I said '*What!*' because he whacked his sheepskin gloves together, laughed, and bowing low in an exaggeration of gentlemanliness, pointed me to the stile over the fence. The old snow that back in the village had been pummelled into black furry lumps by boots and tyres was here white and pure and endless to either side of the narrow path. As I hoiked myself over and landed on the moor, the new fall became suddenly denser and began to swirl down around us on diagonal funnels of air. Looking across the landscape I felt as if we two were inside one of those glass paperweights that had been shaken and set down.

He came up beside me and looked down with amusement from beneath his red knit hat. 'I thought you'd like that.'

I said, 'You wouldn't be willing to run that past me again, would you?'

The amusement brightened another ten watts. 'I've been asked to go out to Managua for six months. The Sandinista government have invited a group of European doctors to advise on the setting up of a national health service.'

It was what I thought he'd said.

'How on earth . . . ?'

'My articles – the ones that were reprinted in the *International Journal of Progressive Medicine*.' A grin broke out.

'But it's *hot* out there,' said a high squeaky variation on my voice. 'You'll hate it.'

He raised a gloved index finger. 'Not in the autumn and winter.'

Oh no, I thought, he'll be gone *then*, just at the time . . .

I stooped to pick up a stone from the path. 'You going to say yes?' I asked. I'd gotten my tone back down and just prayed it sounded light.

He shrugged – I caught him out of the corner of my eye as I pitched the stone into the snow with a feeble underhand pitch.

'I'm thinking about it. All of us who've been invited are meant to be getting together to discuss it the week after next over in Göteborg.'

I stared out at the landscape again and this time it looked bleak and foreboding. (He would be away *then*.)

From behind me I heard him say, 'My flight leaves at eight on the Monday morning. I'll have to come down the night before and stay over in town.'

I cleared my throat, remembered my manners. 'Oh, un hunh – good,' I heard myself mumble from a long way off. I wasn't going to be able to keep this up (*then*); the time had come to head back. I turned.

David didn't move and there was no trace now of any amusement, either in his eyes or around his mouth. 'Maybe we can get together.'

The casualness was faked – I could hear the effort he'd put into it – and what I should have said, what I ought to have said immediately to help the poor sod relax, was yes, sure, great, I'd love to.

For a long time, though, I seemed to have lost all ability to speak. (*What a bloody time to pick*.) And when I finally recovered it, when at long last the 'sh' of the sure was at the point of pushing its way through the bite of my front teeth, a gust of iced moor wind suddenly lifted the top layer off the surrounding snow, whirled it up round us, and dropped it down the cracks between my neck and my scarf, my socks and my shoes, my gloves and my cuffs. A frozen fist seemed to grab hold of the base of my spine, setting off a chill which shuddered up my back and climaxed as it reached the middle of my shoulder blades.

Four

My breath, I notice suddenly, is making white clouds in the air. My body is so frozen into its crouch position that if it weren't for an abrupt flare-up of indignation (*how dare they keep me in these conditions*) I wouldn't even be trying to straighten my poor stiff back.

How *dare* they.

Upright at last I cross the three yards to the door and give the knob what seems like a pretty hard twist. But my hard is not hard enough for what is unquestionably a lock.

Could I jimmy it with a credit card? I search the room with my eyes for my handbag – the top of the dresser, the side of the chair, the underneath of the bed – but see neither it nor my shoes. What I do spy is the paperback jacket of *A Marx Reader* on the bedside table. If the lock is a Yale, this might serve in place of a credit card. I've got to try.

More slowly now, one careful foot in front of the other, I walk over to the book, pick it up and walk back with it to the door. When I try to fiddle the lock, however, I fail, not because of my returning enervation or because the corners of the cover are too soft from use to slip into the crack, but because the lock is a mortice.

I give the knob another twist, then slap the doorframe with my palm. This sounds about as powerful as a fish flapping in its death-throes; it also makes my palm sting like hell.

Can I summon the necessary emotion to stomp my foot – *make* then come for me? I'm working on it when I hear a new sound from below. A door opening and closing? A moment later, water in the pipes. Again comes the opening and closing noise, then, silence.

I strain to listen, my ear pressed against the door.

More water in the pipes: a flushing toilet.

I reconnect with my bladder, checking, and in the course of this become aware of a sensation of stickiness at the top of my inner thighs. I somehow crane my neck around to see the back of myself, looking for a sign of staining. A half thought rises, a half memory (*it can't be a period; how can it be a period?*), then distraction comes on an upwind: the smell of burning toast.

I close my eyes, feel the saliva rise around my tongue, am about to be transported into visions of ecstatic breakfasts I have known, when a thump sounds beyond the curtains: the outer door. Moved by what feels like the end of my energy, I recross the room and peer out again past the side edge of the curtain. Dawn has begun its erosion of night, and the street, just becoming visible beneath shadow, is deserted. A soft mizzle shimmers past the yellow light of the street lamp.

As I stare out, a figure emerges from the extreme right and walks slowly along the opposite pavement into the middle of my field of vision. As it is pausing at the kerb, looking one way, then the other, car headlights swing into the street and catch it in their high beams.

It wears glasses, is medium height, bald, dressed in black, and I think I see a white dog-collar.

The lights dim, change angle. The car inches along so slowly that for a time I can't quite decide whether I'm just hallucinating its movement.

The figure does not cross the road but stays on the pavement and keeps walking until only a hint of white collar is visible; then it fades completely.

The car rolls into the light of the street lamp – it's a dark sedan – and I see the antenna on its front hood and the aerial on the back. I know without a demonstration that it is equipped with a removable flashing bubble light, for its roof, and a button which when you press it lets out either ne-naw ne-naw or whoop whoop whoop.

As it disappears back into darkness I find myself focusing on the window I'm looking out of. These thin transparent panes, it now occurs to me, are all that separate me from the outside world. I test the clasp: it isn't locked.

(*But it's three storeys down.*)

Rain begins to splash gently against the glass as I weigh my lingering dopeyness and fear of the height against my fear of my gaolers. Another small surge of adrenalin makes my mind up for me: I undo the clasp and slowly raise the loose sash window nice-and-easy-does-it. Then even more slowly I lift my right leg to the sill; stick the ankle through the hole to the outside air; push the calf out behind it. When the back of my knee is resting on the ledge I look down and, as my stomach begins to rise, the bells of a distant church start to toll the first mass.

I

I heard the chapel bells about a mile before we reached the St Mary Magdalene Catholic School for Girls; they rang out not simply across distance but across time. This is no tape recording, they declared; there are humans here pulling ropes, making their shoulders ache for this sound.

I'd always thought of southwest Scotland as the moory bit before the Highlands, so the varying terrain between Dumfries and the school, which was on the side of a small hill within sight of Solway Firth, had come as an unexpected pleasure. The snow had stopped exactly at Gretna Green, as if the Scots had refused to take delivery, and after the unending vista of white through the Pennines and Cumberland, the rainlogged greens and browns of the landscape seemed as vibrant as the hot pinks and lemon yellows of the Caribbean.

The young nun who picked me up in the antique school minibus detoured to give me a sight of the house where Robbie Burns wrote Auld Lang Syne. ('All our American visitors like to go here,' she said, perceiving that I'd arrived without doing any homework.) She also told me about the school, which was on the site of a convent built in the fifteenth century by a Catholic noble for his mother and his widowed sister. Mary Queen of Scots had slept there a hundred years later, but not long afterwards it had been closed down by royal order. The oldest structure on the grounds now was the chapel – 'It's just seventeenth century,' she apologised; everything else, including the ten-foot high wall surrounding the enclave that looked as if it had been erected to keep out dragons during the Crusades, was late Victorian reconstruction. I assured her that I wasn't that fussy.

The Mother Superior's office was behind the chapel, but as a mass had started and my escort was eager to get to it, I let myself be led past and up several flights of stairs and along a corridor to the oak-panelled waiting room, where another young woman took charge of my comfort. I had just been handed a cup of tea and a biscuit when Mother Elizabeth opened her door.

'Welcome,' she said, gesturing me in.

Who was it she reminded me of? Oh, of course: my old Girl Scout leader, twenty years ago. She had that same stout, sturdy frame straining the seams of the same nurses'-style uniform, the solid sensible shoes, the short grey hair. Add the light behind the eyes, the good humour in the corners of the mouth and you had a woman who would probably as soon fix roofing tiles and mend plumbing as preach piety – so I fancied anyway.

She pointed me to a dark wood and leather chair with a straight high back. It was positioned beside the window overlooking a deserted play area that was shiny with a skin of moisture where it wasn't puddled. Behind it I made out a winter vegetable garden.

As she sat behind her desk I retrieved a photo of Annie Murphy from my bag and handed it across to her.

'Ay, that's Anne Marie,' she said, her smile fond. 'She lived here for eleven years – stayed on a year after her O levels, then went off to train as a nurse. That was nearly six years ago.' She handed me back the photo. 'I didn't want to pry over the telephone, but might I ask why she's hired you? Is she in some kind of trouble?'

Clearly the police hadn't been in touch.

I sighed and leaned towards her. 'I have – rather bad news,' I said.

She looked into my eyes a moment, then nodded. I heard the worrying of beads. 'How?' she asked.

I told her and when I'd finished she closed her eyes and began to move her lips silently. I waited and eventually her attention returned.

'What can I do to help you find the unhappy soul who's done this?'

'Fill in some of the background for me. For example, she was badly burned as a child.'

'Yes. She was still being treated when I first met her. Poor wee lass was only six or seven.'

'Did she ever tell you anything about the circumstances?'

She shook her head. 'Not me; not the doctor – no one.'

'Do you think she *remembered* what happened?'

'I'm certain she did. She had terrible nightmares until she was a teenager.' She gestured a hug. 'She'd cry her eyes out sometimes, it made your heart break listening.'

'But she didn't talk about it.'

'Never.'

'How about her parents?'

She shook her head again. 'I've always presumed they died at the time.'

I got out the old photograph of the very young Annie walking beside the slender woman of about twenty-five.

She took it from me and stared into it. 'Yes. This is the one she used to keep beside her bed. That was her mother.'

'Good, I hoped that's who she was . . . Now, I wonder, would it be possible to check her enrolment records?'

She sighed. 'It wouldn't I'm afraid. Anne Marie was already a boarder here when I took over from Mother Josephine, God rest her soul, and the filing system in those days was . . .' she paused to select the politest phrase, ' "more informal". I'm sorry.'

'It can't be helped. What about visitors; do you recall her having any?'

'Only her foster parents . . . My goodness now, what were they called?' She got up, went across to her filing cabinet, pulled open the middle drawer and almost immediately plucked out a green wallet. She skimmed it as she walked back to the desk. 'Oh yes, of course – they were called Murphy too.'

'Relatives?'

She read some more. 'I have no note of that.' She frowned. 'They didn't treat her the way you'd expect a family to treat a young girl. She stayed here with us during the holidays every year as far as I can remember.'

'Do you have their address?'

She turned over still more pages and finally withdrew an envelope addressed to 'Joseph and Christine Murphy, 26 Cameron Parade, Glasgow' which had been returned four years before, marked 'Unknown at this address'. 'This is the best I can do.'

I copied it out, taking from her as well a phone number retrieved from an old address book.

'Right,' I said, 'that leaves friends and enemies.'

Her smile indulged my naivety. 'There were fifteen other girls in her year. Who was or wasn't speaking to whom was a besetting and ever-shifting preoccupation for them all.'

'I'd be grateful for their names and last known addresses anyway.'

She obliged and when I had the list I thanked her and said, 'If anything else occurs to you . . .'

'I was just remembering, in fact, how unsurprised I was when she wrote saying she'd become involved with that peace camp near the hospital where she trained. She was quite fearsomely non-violent.'

'Did you save her letters?'

'You mean both postcards?' she smiled. Then she said, 'No, I jest. There must be half a dozen here.'

'May I?'

'Be my guest,' she nodded, handing me the bunch.

Facts unfolded – a trip here, an exam there, a move to a cheaper place, a rise in grant, a job offer, another move, the camp, a promise to phone and visit. The only note with the slightest undercurrent of the unsaid to it was the most recent, sent a year before from Liverpool. 'Unexpected job came up nursing a friend,' it read. 'Hope to be out of here soon.'

Mother Elizabeth knew of no Liverpool connection and called in two younger nuns who'd both taught Annie to see if they remembered any. We talked through their collections of anecdotes for another hour but while my picture of the dead woman gained shading and nuance, my picture of her killer remained undeveloped.

Before I left I tried the old telephone number of the Murphys, but it had been reassigned to someone else two years before. Unpromising a sign as this was, I nevertheless checked my train timetable again and reflected on the fact that I was closer to Glasgow than I was to London: if I went there now and got the investigation of this detail over with, I could reward myself with a flight home.

The blizzard swept in from Iceland via the Butt of Lewis and Inverness just behind the six o'clock southbound flight, which I was on. The winds at our tail were not kind and when we finally touched down at Gatwick my stomach had rolled around so much it no longer knew where it'd started. I caught a taxi without even thinking how much more expensive it was than the train and was in front of my door searching for my key by eight.

As a housekeeper I'm a minimalist – everything, plants included, is low-maintenance – and the appearance of order is enough to satisfy me. In the case of papers and books I don't even demand that, provided they keep to designated mess zones such as the telephone table in the entrance hall just outside the living room.

I was in the middle of taking off my boots when I realised the piles were too neat.

I looked under the table, feeling simultaneously a little paranoid and a little foolish for feeling paranoid. I went into the sitting room and looked at the second major mess zone, the pine bench beside the sofa, then into the bedroom for a look at the desk. Nothing was missing and so far as I could see nothing had been added but both had the same too-neatness. I went back to the hall and took apart the telephone, then checked behind the TV and in the cistern of the toilet. In the end I decided I'd taken sensible precaution as far as it would go, found an old sleeping pill and went to bed.

When I walked into my office the next morning I experienced the sensation of invasion there too and when Claudine came in five minutes later she found me, still in my coat, examining the undersides of each of the file folders stacked every which way on my desk and all over the side table.

'You didn't by any chance tidy up my papers after I left on Friday did you?' I asked her.

'No. Why? What have you lost?'

'I'm not sure. Something just feels a bit wrong.'

'Maybe the cleaner . . .'

But I shook my head. The cleaner knew better. I started to take off my coat.

She watched me with a certain fidgetiness.

'Well?' she said finally, eagerness bouncing up and down in her voice. 'Did you find anything out up north?'

I suddenly realised this case was like *Dallas* or *EastEnders* to her. Forget the usual courtesies of subordinate to superior, like how about a cup of tea your worship. She wanted a fix of the next thrilling instalment.

'Not a lot I couldn't have found out on the telephone.'

'Oh no,' she groaned like a kid who's been told the TV's broken.

'It wasn't a complete waste,' I smiled. 'I went out to a leafy green suburb of Glasgow I'd never heard of before, met some incredibly hospitable people I could hardly understand and managed to establish that the Murphys must have left there at least six years ago. How's your flu?'

'Gone,' she sniffed. But she wasn't that easily deflected. 'The Mother Superior,' she started, 'did you . . . ?'

Just at that moment, however, the receptionist buzzed to warn me that George was about to burst through the door, which he immediately did, all cold air and muddy shoes and tea cosy hat left over from his low couture days. 'Ladies,' he drawled, removing an invisible stetson and bowing first to me, then to Claudine, before continuing on in and taking up his spot beside the heater. It was early in the day for George.

'What do you want first,' he said, loosening his right glove one finger at a time like a show magician, 'the good news or the good news?'

'You choose,' I smiled.

'OK,' he said. 'We've found out an interesting little fact about Tonio Shiraz: he makes regular trips in and out of Iran.'

'Oh?'

'Do you realise what that means?'

'He has good contacts there?'

He nodded. 'His second wife turns out to be the younger half sister of a guy who's big in their armaments mafia.'

'How come he let her marry a goy?'

'Shiraz's father was Muslim. It was her second marriage. I don't know. The point is, Shiraz must have a security services link this end.'

'You're saying he co-operates with MI6?'

'I'm sure he wouldn't be in business if he didn't. And they are one of the few agencies with the contacts to get Shiraz's car phone records wiped.'

'You think they'd help him set up his ex-wife for a manslaughter charge?'

'Who knows. That's Vic Phillips' department.'

I made a note to take it up with him. 'What else?'

'I found the doctor who published that report saying the women at the peace camp are being bombarded with ultra low-frequency sound waves by the American military.'

'And?'

He rifled in his coat pockets, pulled a tobacco pouch from the right one. ' "And" at first he spun me a line: yes he'd seen her around the hospital but no he didn't know her and no he hadn't a clue she'd been one of the camp women who broke into the American base to help provide him with evidence and what was all this about anyway, he thought they'd charged someone with manslaughter.'

'He *organised* the break-ins?' I couldn't believe the women had allowed anyone, especially a man, to . . .

'I didn't say "organised". But certainly collaborated – read his report, you'll see.' He'd finished sprinkling dark flakes on a black liquorice paper and paused to run the point of his tongue along the gum. When he'd rolled the result into a thin stick, he opened his jacket and from the inner breast pocket withdrew an A4 booklet folded lengthwise, which he unfolded not altogether satisfactorily and handed to me. 'He needed insiders. And he didn't deny that. What he did deny was knowing who any of them were except for his link person.' He felt around in his right-hand pocket again, frowned, tried the left.

'Then what happened?'

'I explained to him very clearly the side you're on and what the problem is and what your particular line is on things. I gave him the number where I was staying – told him if he remembered anything else . . .' He began patting the pocket over his heart.

Claudine, who had been hanging around by the door listening, retrieved a box of matches from her bag, struck one and held it out for him. He dipped towards it gratefully.

'I figured,' he said on the inhale, 'it would take him two hours.'

'Two hours for what?' she asked.

'For checking Dee out – checking me out. I forgot it was Saturday: it took him three. We met at a little freehouse way out in the back of beyond – bleeder *insisted* on sitting outside, too.' He shivered.

'And?'

This prompt was from Claudine but it was me he looked over at as his hand once more reached into his inner breast pocket. This time he pulled out one of those thin paper napkins that sit in silver dispensers on pub counters – the kind that are useless for anything but doodling on. What had been doodled on this one was a phone number. 'That's for his link person – woman named Lucy Wiltshire.'

'Great,' I said, taking it from him. 'Thanks.'

George's nod was diffident but there was a suggestion of beadiness in his eye: something else was coming. 'He has a couple of other theories about Annie Murphy's death which he asked me to pass on as well,' he said casually.

'Oh? I've been trying to avoid speculating.'

Claudine said, 'What are they?'

He pretended to examine his fingernails. 'One he says he thinks of as the individual, the other, the collective.'

She frowned.

Warmth rose behind my ears and began to creep towards my cheeks: the truth was, there were certain connections I had been refusing to make. I cleared my throat. 'How does the individual one go?'

He puffed and smiled. 'You want me to sing it for you?'

'I want you to prevent me from wrapping my hands around your throat by telling me.'

The smile widened an infuriating iota.

'Let me guess,' Claudine burst out. 'An American soldier.' She was pretty excited. 'One of them saw her inside the base and – and – I know: she saw him on the street that day – and – and . . .' (Her imagination was struggling now, you could see it on her brow, but would she give up?) '. . . I know: he took her off to blackmail her – and – and . . .'

'Claudine,' I cut in, 'Claudine, hang on. Those American soldiers are in there to guard that base. If one of them was on duty and caught her in there, he wouldn't blackmail her, he'd arrest her.'

She'd become attached to her theory, the way one does. 'Not if he needed money for something.'

'But Annie Murphy was poor – she had no family.'

She opened her mouth, then lifted her knuckle to it, her brow again creased with the intensity of her ruminations.

George said to her, 'Actually you've hit on Wilson's theory, only he put it the other way around. He reckons she could have caught one or two of the soldiers doing something they oughtn't to have been doing when they should have been guarding the missiles – snorting a bit of coke, maybe, or sleeping, maybe sleeping with each other. She *was* in there with a camera.'

My palm went automatically for my forehead. It wasn't physical pain I felt, but still my head hurt. 'I don't fancy proving *that*.'

'Yah, well, as they say, you ain't heard *nuthin'* yet. According to his other theory . . .'

This time I was the one to guess: 'The CIA,' I came out with. I sounded cool and quite serious.

He nodded.

My poor head dropped to my chest. 'Dammit.' This was it, of course, the one I hadn't wanted to contemplate. Nor was the aversion completely irrational or completely to do with my emotional state: I had already had in my legal career one memorable encounter with the security services of my homeland

and had rather hoped that one per legal career was all that got handed out. I said, 'You're supposed to be helping me get Gillian Shiraz acquitted. I need to be able to pin this on someone else *in court*.'

He showed no sign of remorse. 'It's no more difficult to pin it on them than on MI6 – and it's a hell of a lot more appealing than the soldier idea if you ask me.'

Claudine said, 'I don't know. I only met those soldiers once and I can believe it.'

He turned to her. 'It's not credibility that's the problem, it's provability in one lifetime. Do you realise how many soldiers the United States government keeps on that particular air base? Two thousand. Whereas with American intelligence services, there is one motive and it's looking us in the eye: she somehow managed to penetrate their tightest security – a young nurse got right up within telephoto lens distance of a nuclear missile. And look at the quality of the cover-up: it was damn slick, damn professional. It should have worked, too; probably would have in fact if it hadn't been for the old boy downstairs and his personal vendetta against dykes.'

I groaned. (Did I really deserve this? *Again*?)

'Well,' he said, sucking and finding his cigarette had died, 'there's an alternative.' He stubbed it out. 'She could have been a plant *by* the security services who got found out.'

I groaned louder.

'I knew you'd like that one.'

'It's not a time for joking, George. Please.'

His shrug was provocative.

I let myself be provoked. 'But she was among *peace* women,' I protested with some anguish. 'They wouldn't *kill* her.'

'No, but they would cover up an accident.'

I was sure there was a reply to this but I couldn't summon it.

Our weekly office meeting was unusually heated that Monday morning. I wasn't the only one unhappy about the way Nicola had agreed to represent one of the IRA suspects betrayed by the informer Gerard Ryan without going through our procedure for accepting controversial cases. Simone resented being 'bounced', as she put it, because she thought the IRA were a load of thugs and hoodlums who were proof if any were needed that two wrongs don't make a right. Rita, declaring herself indifferent to the moral debate, was concerned simply that, because the IRA were *perceived* as terrorists, involvement in a case of this kind could damage our reputation with victims of violence. In Maggie's opinion the IRA were victims of violence themselves – 'freedom fighters engaged in a just war against colonial oppressors'; her irritation arose because Nicola's practical legal experience was limited to property conveyancing, which meant she was going to need back-up support, which would inevitably mean more work for Maggie, and she would have appreciated being asked first.

Nicola, to give her credit, bore up well for about half an hour. She dropped her initial approach, which was to tell us how honoured we should feel, looked down at her hands, and muttered contrite apologies at appropriate intervals. Even I started to feel sympathy for her. Then, suddenly, something about the tone or the length of the proceedings must have pricked her because she sat upright and, tapping the table with her index finger, started accusing us of not briefing her properly about our 'stupid bloody procedures' in the first place. My imminent sympathy vanished: *I'd* explained those stupid bloody procedures to her myself her first day. Indignantly I leaned across the table to say so.

Suze, who'd managed thus far to sit back from the discussion, was at last drawn in. 'Yes – well – there have obviously been a number of misunderstandings. The point is that an alleged IRA member has been charged with crimes, is pleading not guilty, and has hired this firm to defend her. Our name is now on her legal aid application and I think we have to agree to let Nicola carry on with it. While it's true that it's outside her normal field, she follows Irish politics and she came here to expand her experience. Anyway, it's not as if there's a queue of solicitors eager for IRA cases. I'm willing to support her when I'm available.' She looked at Maggie. 'Would you do it when I'm not?'

Maggie looked a bit grudging but nodded.

We talked for another ten minutes about how the communications breakdown had occurred and how to ensure it didn't happen again. Everyone gradually came around to Suze's view, though just before we made it formal I said, 'There's one final guarantee I think we need: we must be informed before statements are made to the media.'

Nicola put her hand on her heart. 'That's fine by me.'

II

When I came out of the meeting, one of my clients was sitting in reception flicking through the pages of the *Law Review*. As soon as she saw me she was on her feet and by my side: her eldest son had been picked up truant from school. They said he was dealing drugs to younger children, they said he'd resisted arrest. They were holding him at Tottenham police station and could I go there and get him out, *please* could I? I hoped in fact I wouldn't need to go there – I had so much paperwork to do – but after several long time-wasting phone calls, I admitted defeat, got into a cab with her and went.

This little drama ate up the rest of the morning, cut through lunch and was whittling away on early afternoon before it was resolved with his release. It left me feeling as if my whole energy quota for the week had been sucked out of me in one great slurp: I was limp and floppy and yearned for bed. I almost obeyed the impulse, too, but just as my feet were heading off home I remembered the list of things I'd been supposed to get through and pictured what would happen to my tomorrow if all of it were left over. I ended up stopping into a takeaway kebab place for a little cup of Turkish coffee that looked like camel slurry and didn't taste much better, but the jolt of caffeine got me through the motions of a certain pressing bit of personal business (I could only bear that euphemism) and back to the office.

By then it was half past three and I was again feeling so crappy that I knew I had to be putting out a great black cloud of no-go zone. Claudine certainly kept well back, just mugged a grim smile and handed me more papers for my collection – telephone messages, incoming mail, letters for signing. I bent my head down over the stack and was flipping through and skimming as I opened my door, went in, closed it behind me, and started to cross to my desk.

A throat cleared and, startled, I stopped and looked up. Suze was standing in the frame of the interconnecting door between our two offices.

'Hi!' she said. She was excited about something, this was obvious from the grin, the silly wave, the lolloping way she approached, like a retriever puppy.

'Hi!' I said, but I felt myself backing off from her. Goddammit, I thought, she knows me. Can't she see I'm whacked, want (need) to be alone for a few minutes? Why doesn't she leave me be?

But I knew her too; when she got like that, you had to let her burst and bubble over, even if you didn't like it.

She sat down on the edge of the chair beside my desk and continued to grin at me while I slipped out of my coat, dropped it over the desk, fell heavily into my own chair.

'Your murder case,' she started in, able to wait no longer.

I pulled back further from her without being able to help it. 'I had a wasted weekend,' I told her. Why was I going along with this? I would say something I regretted, I could sense it. 'Look,' I began, thinking to warn her about my mood, 'Suze . . .'

But her inner gun had sounded and she was off. 'I know,' she said, 'Claudine told me all about it.' She shook her head, then fixed me in the eye with a significant glance. 'She told me about your conversation with George this morning, too.'

'Oh,' I said. It was a leaden noise, flat as rolled tarmac.

She didn't notice. 'I had a quick look in Annie's box of things,' she confided.

I pressed my top teeth into my bottom lip. She had a right to do this, I reminded myself; she was the other partner in the firm and she had a right to do it. Moreover it was the kind of case I'd have normally told her more about than she'd have wanted to know. And of course she'd never had a murder case: her Miss Marple was stirring.

Why was I being so horrid?

She stood up, went over to the box, retrieved — what? The old novel? Yes.

She carried it back to me. 'Did you see *this*?'

I nodded.

'Do you know what it is?'

'A novel.'

She was too engrossed even to groan. 'Have you *read* it?'

I shook my head.

'Well,' she said, straightening into her Expert posture, 'it was withdrawn from sale here when I was doing my law exams back in '72. It tells *exactly* how to put together several kinds of explosive devices.'

'Suze,' I started again, a little more forcefully, 'look, honestly, I'm not feeling very . . .'

She put her palms on my desk and leaned towards me. 'I have a theory,' she announced.

I sighed. Suze might heap sarcasm on *my* inspirations, but the truth was she was second only to George in her love of theories.

'No – really – I mean it – listen to me,' she protested. 'It involves these facts:' – she held up her thumb as number one – 'this book'; she held up her index finger – 'the postcard of the American bases, ringed in red ink'; her middle finger – 'her name'; her ring finger – 'and the news references to a certain sequence of arrests which started the day Annie Murphy disappeared.' She smiled and waited a full half second. 'Got it?'

I had in fact caught an extremely faint scent of 'it', which I instantly rejected. 'No,' I said.

She was leaning again. 'OK, OK, here's a hint: the CIA. Ask yourself this, Dee: what would American intelligence want with a bona fide peace woman?'

There was a rumbling beneath my crust of restraint and a crack suddenly appeared. 'I thought you had a *new* idea,' I said with sharp impatience. 'If you're going to start trying to persuade me that she was really an undercover agent of the American government . . .'

She shook her head. 'No, not that. I'm serious. Think about it. Why would they go after a genuine peace woman?'

'Because she broke into their bloody base.'

Still oblivious to my irritation, she peered at me with a wizened squint. 'Fifty women must have broken into that base. Five times that many must have broken into Greenham.'

'*She* took photographs of soldiers and missiles.'

She shrugged the shrug of a New York Yiddish grandmother. 'Photos are nothing. What's important is who she took them for – what that organisation was going to do with them.'

I thought, Whoa – whoa here now, steady up. Enunciating with slow care, I said to her, 'Suze if you are driving at what I think you could be driving at, I think you should stop right . . .'

But she wasn't paying attention. She was too busy opening the old novel first to its front cover, then to its back – lifting it upside down like a bird with its wings out – giving it a shake. A folded sheet of paper eased out of the pages and dropped on to my desk. She picked it up and handed it to me. I unfolded it and found myself looking at a photocopy of a printed poem.

'Recognise it?' she asked me.

'Well it's not Milton and it's not Shakespeare and it's sure as hell not Sylvia Plath.'

She took it back and waved it at me. 'Bobby Sands. IRA hunger striker, died in prison in 1981 in protest over . . .'

'I *know* who Bobby Sands is,' I snapped. Outrage raced up my body, jerking it to its feet, filling in the pockets where energy used to be. 'And how dare you, how *dare* you. Annie Murphy gave up a lot for that peace camp. She may have given up her life for it for all I know. The last thing she'd have died for was a violent group like the IRA. That *is* what you're implying, isn't it? . . . Well? Isn't it?'

She looked right into my eye. 'People are not always what they appear,' she said, very low and now enunciating carefully herself. 'As you well know.'

That did it. On top of everything else, she was sticking the knife in. My hands leapt to my hips, pushing into them hard. 'Just because I've been taken in by someone in the past doesn't mean my judgment is *useless*. It doesn't mean I'm a permanently gullible na-na . . .'

'I wasn't suggesting . . .'

'And who are you to talk anyway, Suze Aspinall? You haven't exactly scored a hundred per cent in the assessment-of-honest-characters sweepstakes yourself lately.' She made appeasing gestures with her hands but I'd found my flow. 'In fact if you ask me, which you haven't had the courtesy to do, I think you've got a cheek coming in here spinning fantasies about a case that I've had very little support from you on at all.'

'Come on Dee,' she said, beginning to get heated up herself, 'that's not fair. I'm not *here* very much. I'm chairing a police committee, remember?'

'The police committee hasn't been taking you off for leisurely lunches and celebrity lawyer spots on the radio.'

That did it. She flared. 'I've heard enough of this . . .'

'Yeah, well, I haven't. I'm still waiting for an apology.'

Her hands were now pushing hard into *her* hips. 'For what? Just answer me that – for what? For leaving you alone? Dee, who asks who to lunch? Who asks who over to dinner? Who's been worried like hell about this tetchy mood you've been in ever since you split up with David? Who's bloody your *friend* in here in case you've forgotten?'

A sceptical grunt escaped me, quite unreasoning I'm sure.

She burst out into flailing semaphore: 'OK, OK, so maybe I misjudged Nicola Steyning a bit. Why do you have to rub my nose in it? I don't bloody rub yours in your mistakes.' Her hands clasped each other in impatient prayer as she raised her eyes and implored the ceiling. 'Jesus, I just wish to God I knew what's wrong with you lately. You're paranoid, you're unpleasant, you're alway preoccupied, you're . . .'

'. . . pregnant.'

'Pregnant . . .' There her voice caught and she looked at me dumbly; I watched her face blanch from high red to bloodless. 'Pregnant?' Her hand went to her mouth, which slackened at the touch. 'Oh *Dee*.'

I slumped back down into my chair, my forehead bent over my desk.

'What are you going to do?'

I shook my head and made myself confide to her where I'd gone on my way back from the police station. Unfortunately I must have mumbled this confession into my blotter.

She came around beside me, sat down on the arm of my chair, put her hand on the middle of my back. 'What was that?' she asked me gently.

My eyes were filling and I blinked hard as I lifted my head. 'I stopped in – into the Well-Woman clinic at – at Warren Street. I – I'm going to go in and – and have a talk about it on Thursday.'

She sighed a long and pained sigh and rubbed my back a couple of times. 'Do you think you might have it?'

I shook my head again, not to say 'No' but to say 'Don't know – haven't any idea.'

'David . . . ?'

I kept shaking my head that same way, until I realised how heavy it was becoming; then I told her about seeing him in Yorkshire and the uncertainties I'd had and how I'd ended up not telling him. 'I can't picture me raising a child,' I heard myself admit in the end. It sounded like a terrible truth.

Her nod was sympathetic. 'I know the problem.'

'And do you still worry?'

She knew what I meant. 'That I'm not a real woman?' She shrugged. '*I* know I'm not Jack Lemmon in drag.'

'It's the *outer* pressure I'm talking about. Eighty-five or ninety per cent of the female population has children.'

'Yes, and they're constantly trying to get you to join them. In fact it's fair to say that the pressure gets worse. Wait till you get to my age.' Suze was four years older than me – nearing forty. 'Suddenly women who've never seemed the slightest bit interested turn out to be secretly desperate. You feel incredibly churlish for not feeling the same.'

'And you don't?'

She made a *comme-ci*, *comme-ça* gesture with her hand. 'I'd be lying if I said no and lying if I said yes. I think of it as my hormones' last call. Fortunately Peter provides me with a good excuse for not giving in. He's quite positive: he's had one family and doesn't want another.' She grinned. 'Why are we talking about me? I've always said I'd be a terrible mother – what a lot of work! Whereas you – you'd be good.'

I grunted ungraciously.

'I mean it.'

'Come on, if I had any kind of vocation for mothering, I'd have done it years ago.'

'Not necessarily. There are late starters in every field who are brilliant.'

'Well what about overpopulation then? What about the planet?'

'If every two people only created one new person, the planet would be fine.'

'Suze for heaven's sake – you're supposed to be telling me why I *shouldn't* have it!'

'Am I? Gosh, thanks for telling me honey bun,' she said in her bad mock-American. Then she looked at her watch. 'Look – I know. Why don't you come home with me tonight? His eminence is out at a meeting and I've got the fixings for Aspinall Chicken Khorma à la Sharwoods. If you pick up a bottle of Bulgaria's best, that should do us. You fancy it?'

Fancy it, my God! Suze had a wonderful sink-in sofa everyone knew as the womb: enveloped in that, with a half a bottle down me, talking in the afterglow of curry à la Sharwoods – it was exactly what I needed.

I said, 'I really ought to go out to bloody Moleham this evening and talk to this woman Lucy Wiltshire. Annie didn't cut through the fence and go into the base several times on her own. A group of them went in and I need to be sure the rest of them are all right. If it turns out they are, I need to know if Lucy or any of them can explain why Annie was singled out – preferably with evidence. I don't frankly need any more theories at this point. I need a solid lead. I need . . .'

She pointed an index finger upwards. 'You need company.' She directed the tip of it to her chest. 'I am not expected home. I'll give you a lift out there.' Then she crooked the finger into a knuckle, which she used to push the phone across the desk my way.

You need at least a little luck from time to time in this work and a piece got doled out to me when my call to Lucy caught her on her way out the door. It held when she agreed to see me. Then she gave me a choice: I could wait until she got back the end of the week, or I could meet her on Salisbury Plain, where she was headed.

I put my hand over the mouthpiece to ask Suze what she thought. Her long almond eyes expanded as if some luck had just been doled out to her too, and when she'd least been expecting it. 'Are the American missiles *out*?' she asked me.

I nodded. 'Apparently a convoy left Greenham Common on a practice alert three nights ago. It's meant to be "hiding" in a copse of trees on Salisbury Plain somewhere. There's a big demonstration going on she says.'

Suze's smile competed with her eyes in wideness. 'Do you know I've always wanted to see one of these exercises? I mean how on earth do they hide half a dozen missile launchers, or however many it is they take out for airings, in the countryside?' She pointed at the phone. 'Fix an exact spot with her. There's eight miles of that plain.'

We agreed to meet at the car park opposite Stonehenge between seven and half-past.

This early luck seemed to abandon us after that, though. First an accident at Baker Street delayed us getting to my place; then, in the ten minutes it took to fetch some warmer, rougher clothes, rain started, fat filthy gobbets of it. All along Marylebone Road up over the Westway we crept, and once we edged our way to the other side things didn't improve, only now we were jammed in among three lanes. One way and another it took us two hours just to get past Heathrow.

Neither of us actually minded this – we had an awful lot to say to each other – and in fact the only reason we fell silent like we did just past Andover was because of the way the rain thickened into sleet and began to come at the windscreen horizontally. We inched along the A303 at about fifteen mph, guided through the swirling tunnel of flakes and the invisible landscape by the iridescent white road line picked out by the right headlight. We were over an hour late with maybe half an hour to go; I was squinting ahead through the squeaking windshield wipers into the enveloping darkness with as much concentration as Suze. Suddenly and at the same moment we saw a speck of red in the distance and as she touched her foot down on the brake I pressed mine to the floor sympathetically. The speck enlarged as we moved slowly closer, enlarged and kept enlarging, then distinguished itself as a diminishing line of brake lights: we pulled up behind the last in the line, which didn't even seem to have its engine running. Suze muttered, undid her seat belt, yanked up the hand brake, opened her door, got out. Leaning into the wind, she walked through the icy downpour to the car in front, peered into its side window, shrugged at me, pointed up the road, and walked on to the next car. I lost sight of her after that and was deliberating about getting out to follow when she reappeared.

'Police road block,' she said, brushing snow off her coat as she got back in.

'What for?'

She let out a single syllable laugh that said 'You need ask?'

'The missile convoy?' I guessed. When she nodded I said, 'But it can't be later than nine. Surely it's much too early for it to be on the road? I thought they only moved the things around in the dead of night.'

'Not, apparently, when the temperature is going to drop as far as they're predicting it's going to drop tonight.' She gave me one of her defy-*this*-if-you-dare looks: 'I want to go watch it go by,' she stated. 'The junction to the Stonehenge road's only about a quarter of a mile up. We'll be able to see the car park from there. You into walking?'

I had put on several layers: thermal tights, thick socks, boots, jeans, two sweaters, a coat – but I felt frail and cold just listening to the wind gusting outside us, and reluctant to push myself. 'Just leave the car parked here you mean?'

She turned off the ignition. 'Sure,' she said. 'Everyone else's done it.'

By now another car was idling behind us, eyes peering out of the front window as we'd peered, trying to work out what was going on. Two more were coming up the roadway in our direction.

I forced myself out and Suze pretended to lock the long-broken doors of her banged-up old Mini. Then we walked along the edge of the road, between the roadside and the line of cars, towards the junction.

It took us nearly twenty minutes.

The junction was closed by flares and by a line of police cars. Individual officers, kitted out in dark, overlarge plastic macs with hoods, were milling around.

The sleet had stopped and beyond the blockade I could just make out the stones of the ancient site sitting minutely on the distant horizon. Constable's painting of the same scene a hundred and fifty years earlier came to mind – the tall rocks, four or five times the height of a human, jutting out of the field, backed by storm clouds and a double rainbow. Some of that drama had still been there fifteen years before, when I'd first come here; there hadn't been a fence, anyway. And there certainly hadn't been a police blockade.

The rhythmic shush of nylon sliding against nylon made us both turn as a male officer approached. Who were we, he wanted to know, and what were we doing here? When Suze told him, he instructed us to go back to our car and head off on a long circuitous maze of B-roads. Arguers by profession, we challenged his authority to make us do any such thing. He didn't much like this and was working up to put his side again when a loud noise, the noise of an engine, made us all stop talking and look out towards the road. A single white headlight emerged, then two more behind it, then four more. The volume of engine sound became louder and louder. Motorcycle police, a whole battalion (or whatever unit they come in) neared – took over the road – there must have been twenty of them. Behind them there appeared police vans and police buses, one, two, four, six, eight of each. And then, at last, behind these, the American military vehicles began to appear.

Our inquisitor vanished, leaving us alone behind the barricade of his colleagues to watch the approaching procession: two long supply trucks, four jeeps, two vans pulling trailers, a bus pulling a trailer, a bus without a trailer, more jeeps, all of them painted in splotchy camouflage design. Then, after this interminable column, there came into view at last the nose of a vast truck that could only have been one of the missile carriers that all this was about. And no sooner had this first nose showed itself than a cry like the whoops of the Indians charging the cavalry in an old film rose into the air from the other side of the road. Just as suddenly the vast truck braked and came to a stop. The police forming the barricade in front of us rushed off into the road; the shouting grew louder. I looked at Suze, she looked at me and slowly we walked in the direction of the commotion.

Women, most of them on their own, were breaking through the police blockade on the other side – coming out on to the road –

lying down in front of the first missile carrier. Police officers were moving at them in pairs, picking them up by the underarms and ankles, hauling them back to the opposite side of the road, though as fast as they would get rid of one, another two would lie down. A crowd of supporters, holding up candles, chanted louder and louder, an uproar of anti-nuclear chants.

Despite the huge police and military presence, it was possible to walk right up to the trucks carrying the missiles. I did it myself – stood within two feet of an explosive force that I knew was equal to probably twenty Hiroshimas. It filled me with shame. (They had taught me, blessed are the peacemakers.) And then I thought, why would They persecute Annie Murphy – *kill* her – for taking a picture of this thing, this vehicle, that I can practically reach out and touch? It makes no sense.

It was ten before the road was clear enough for this the main part of the convoy to join the vehicles that were supposedly protecting it. It was to be stopped another three times on its journey back to the American base – so we heard later on the news – but the junction we'd been waiting to cross was unblocked at last. We walked back to the car and moved off with the line towards the car park, now three hours late for our meeting.

Where we'd anticipated a lone car waiting for us, people in their hundreds had of course gathered. We cruised slowly, asking everywhere for Lucy, and after establishing that we didn't mean Birmingham Lucy (the tall one with red hair), or Canadian Lucy, or Lucy with the gappy teeth, we found her at the far end of the lot, sitting in a car with five other women, hoping we'd find her. They wanted a drink and I yearned to thaw beside a heater, so we headed off for the one pub that welcomed peace demonstrators.

It was a small mock-Tudor place on a side road beyond a village I'd never heard of and it was already crowded when we got there. Everyone was high on the success of the demonstration, whose triumphs were evidently becoming legend even as we squeezed through the middle of a maze of excited conversations. Wiltshire Lucy (for I'd realised this was how she was actually styled) got involved in her share of these herself, and by the time we made our way through to the bar and escaped with our complement of double brandies, the only standing room was beneath the TV and just to one side of a game of darts.

I watched Lucy as she was caught up in yet another thrilled hug. From her eyes I'd have guessed her age to be maybe twenty-five or twenty-six, but the glow of the unkind lighting showed up lines of experience that suggested she was nearer forty. She was also about five foot ten, so when she finally turned her warm smile on me and said 'Right then – Annie', I was aware of having to look up.

I gave her a little summary of what I knew and what I was after, then I asked her how many times the two of them had broken into the base at Moleham Heath together.

'Six,' she said.

'Always together?'

She nodded.

'You know she took photos inside the base?'

Another nod. 'We all took photos when we could get hold of cameras.'

'I want to know if any individual soldier, American or British, had any personal reason to have it in for her.'

Lucy smiled a sudden enormously amused smile that said I didn't realise what I'd just said. 'I can think of about a platoon that aren't too fond of any of us.'

'And who know your names? Know where to find you?'

Her head moved one way, then another, as if she were hearing the questions from different angles. 'Eh,' she said finally. 'Maybe half.'

Suze fixed on her with that piercing look she has. 'Seriously,' she said.

Lucy had a similar look in her repertoire. 'I *am* serious,' she said. Then, after a pause: 'I could probably put them in order of likelihood, actually.' Another pause. 'And I expect it's me and this other woman, Bea, that they most have it in for. We tend when we see them to go right up to them. Jude, Jenny, Barbara, Helen – they all tend to go for cover. Annie used to go with them.'

'So you don't stay together when you're inside?'

'Are you joking? We've been trying to find equipment that could be anywhere.'

'So Annie could have found something or seen something or heard something that none of the rest of you would know about?'

She frowned as if I'd just released a stink bomb. '*Could* have, sure – anything's possible.'

'But?'

'But she was just a trainee when it came to break-ins, if you know what I mean – a learner. Me, I know what happens when they catch you somewhere you shouldn't be; I know what I have to do and I can do it. But it took me probably a couple of years. Annie – I don't know, she was gutsy – she could walk on tiptoe across dry twigs and not make a sound – but I just don't see it.' She shrugged. 'Not that my instincts are necessarily up to much.' Then she said: 'Anyway, why would she want to do that?'

Now Suze shrugged. 'Maybe she wasn't exactly who she seemed.'

Lucy made a dismissive wave with her hand. 'Not the old infiltration theory?' She rolled her eyes.

But Suze was not to be put off. 'The very openness of the way you run the camp – someone could certainly take advantage of you if they wanted.'

Sarcasm twisted her smile. 'The KGB? The CIA? Boss? The Israelis? The INLA or some other Irish faction? The Workers' Revolutionary Party? Who?'

'Any or all of the above.'

Lucy shook her head in a way that stated clearly how pathetic she found that. 'You know where that theory started, don't you? In *The Sun*, three years ago. Then it got on the radio and a couple of the upmarket dailies put it in their gossip columns. Our choice was to set up an elaborate vetting procedure or forget it. Vetting people is part of the way the world of men operates; that kind of suspicion and mistrust isn't part of the world at the camp. We voted to ignore it. The only time it comes up now is when someone from the media decides to dig it up. Anyway, what's there to learn? And if people like that can infiltrate, it proves our point even more: this is no way to protect a weapon that could destroy the whole planet.' She raised her glass and took the final swallow.

I glanced around, looking for a clock, and my eyes alighted briefly on the television screen, skipped past it, then were wrenched back.

'Oh God,' I said, clutching Suze's bicep.

She turned to me, a frown of concern on her face. 'What's wrong? Are you ill?'

I managed to point to the screen. The interviewer was just putting the microphone to the mouth of Nicola Steyning, who was smiling, her lips already parted over those long teeth in readiness. 'My client,' she said to those millions across the length and breadth of England, Scotland, Ireland and Wales who watch the last news bulletin on independent television, 'my client does not deny her support for the IRA. What she does deny is that the cache of explosives allegedly found in the cupboard of her flat was put there by her.'

From behind me came the sound of forehead meeting palm.

The message from Vic Phillips waiting for me in the office the next morning said, 'Ring me at home first thing.' Just as he answered, though, the baby started to cry in total anguish next to the mouthpiece and when Vic asked me to hang on and dropped the phone, he sounded not far off that condition himself.

I thought about the conversation Suze and I had had on the drive back the night before, about babies and how I'd never seriously ever wanted one and why I was considering it now. This time she'd taken the devil's role. Think about the noise, she'd said; think about the dependency. I'd admitted to feeling guilty for letting the accident happen – the message of the Freudian overtones seemed so blatant. Yes, she'd said, but did I have to have it for that reason? I said I was worried about the emotional afterwaves. She said, Why? Women in Russia and Japan and Sweden have abortions all the time. By the time she dropped me at home I'd seen the line between me, Dee, and the atavistic hormonal mix washing through me, and had decided, or just about, that I wasn't going to have it.

I was congratulating myself on this decision when all went quiet. Vic picked up the phone again. 'I need to see you,' he said. 'It's urgent.'

I explained that I needed to see him urgently too but had this damned emergency office meeting at ten. He reminded me he only lived up the road and hung up before I could protest; ten minutes later in he came. He was wearing a papoose sack on his chest, and the papoose inside it was wrapped up in a pink quilted eskimo suit. I peered around at her face, which was closed in perfect sleep, but felt not the slightest twinge.

Vic didn't want to talk in the office, he wanted me to join them on a walk, and refused even to shed a glove, never mind sit down while I finished my coffee. Instead he reached over to the back of the door for my coat and scarf, which he then held out for me. When I relented and put everything back on, he headed out the door and set off up the Parkway, past Albany Street and into the back of Regent's Park through Gloucester Gate, striding ahead on legs ten inches longer than mine. There was a wooden bench by the entrance to the play area, which was full of squeally toddlers watched over by assorted grown-ups doing clog-dance steps against the early morning chill, and it was here that he finally stopped and sat down.

He'd pulled out a box of Winstons and stuck one in his mouth by the time I took the space beside him; when I said I didn't want one, thanks anyway, he lit up and put the packet in his pocket. Then he flicked some imagined ash off his daughter's shoulder. She was still asleep. 'Gillian Shiraz's arrest wasn't reported by the media,' he told me in a voice just loud enough to penetrate the noise, 'because the Home Office put a D-notice on the story.'

The bit of me raised on the First Amendment baulked as usual. 'They censored it? Why?' But the question was no sooner out of my mouth than an answer occurred to me. 'Oh dear,' I said. 'I think I may know a reason why. Tonio Shiraz: George reckons he probably freelances for the security services on his way back and forth through the Middle East – if so, they may have helped him cover up for himself.'

He didn't like the smell of that, you could tell by the way he wrinkled his nose. 'My man's in F section – internal subversion only.' His tone was ironic. 'What you're talking about is MI6's domain.'

'Come on, he must know people in MI6.'

He looked up through the trees at the sky and addressed an invisible observer: 'Does this mean she's decided I am truly not the dupe of Special Branch?'

I gave him a biff on the knee. 'Vic, be serious. Will you ask him?'

He smiled at me. 'I'll suggest the idea to him and see what kind of response I get – just like I did with your theory about Annie Murphy's death being connected to a story in the morning paper the day she disappeared.'

'You talked about that? What did he say?'

'That he couldn't comment.'

'Damn. I wish you wouldn't look so pleased.'

'But I *am* pleased.' The smile became a grin. 'Maybe it's because I understand the code.'

I opted not to wind him up about his expensive boarding school education; after all, he was trying so hard to be downwardly mobile. 'Are you saying he meant yes?'

The baby started to grizzle and he began to stroke her back with long, slow, downward strokes. 'I'm saying he meant that further exploration of this avenue might prove beneficial.'

'I see. Presumably you pressed him for guidance?'

'It would have been futile and I didn't need it anyway: there's only one story that it could be – and I'm certain the same story is behind the D-notice.'

An inevitability had appeared. 'The arrest of Gerard Ryan,' I heard myself say.

He nodded. 'The connection seems even more plausible if you throw in the fact that Annie Murphy's death has never been reported in the press. It could be *that* that's being censored, not Gillian's arrest. And there's something else as well: the real name of two of the guys Ryan grassed on is Murphy.'

'Vic, half of Ireland must be called Murphy.'

'No more than a quarter, surely. Anyway, one can but try.' He reached under the baby, into his inner coat, took out an envelope and handed it to me. 'It's bare bones stuff, I warn you,' he said. 'Everything I could find in ten minutes on Annie's two namesakes plus all available clippings on Gerard Ryan. What you really ought to do is go over to the North of Ireland – talk to people – see what you can dig up face to face.'

Images rose up – black hoods over heads, eyes and mouth three gaping jack'o'lantern holes; cars burning in the streets; rifles pointing at the world. 'There's a fat chance of that happening,' I said, 'but I'll speak to Theresa – she's got contacts there.'

He shrugged (what I did was up to me), threw down the butt of his cigarette, got to his feet, jiggled the baby. She was waking up now, grizzling seriously, and without thinking I took off a glove and caressed her cheek with a knuckle.

Something inside turned over.

Ignore it. Resist.

I hurried back to the office where I found Rita, Simone and Maggie, all dressed (they said coincidentally) in black, waiting in the board room. Suze, it turned out, had been called away to a private meeting with Nicola, but just as we were taking bets on how long she'd be, in she came.

'Well? What was her excuse?' I wanted to know, too impatient for preliminaries like hello and how are you.

She didn't bother to take off her coat and hat, just pulled out a chair and dropped into it. I saw her jaw clenching and unclenching, which told me she was angry but working on keeping it to herself. 'It emerged,' she said carefully, 'that last night she was shortlisted by the Labour party to fight that by-election outside Manchester. The news was on at teatime, before the meeting, and she needed the publicity.'

All of us clicked our tongues or groaned or muttered incredulous oaths except Simone, who said 'Manchester?'

Suze's nod was weary. 'She says she's going to need to spend at least half her time up there the next ten days. If she's selected she'll move up there for the duration of the campaign.'

Rita made a protesting noise. 'But her work . . .'

'She told me she feels our procedures are too restricting. She has an idea that she can work freelance on her own and asked me to let her take the IRA case with her.'

'But her client's on legal aid,' I said, 'in *the firm's* name . . .'

'I explained that to her. She wasn't very happy with this piece of news. She says she'll apply to amend the legal aid certificate. Meanwhile she's booked to travel over to Belfast on Thursday with Theresa O'Connor to interview possible defence witnesses.'

'Theresa O'Connor?' Maggie asked.

I answered. 'She's representing two of the other ten or twelve

IRA suspects arrested on the word of this senior guy Ryan.'

'Didn't she represent *him* to start with?'

I nodded. 'Until he decided to talk and sacked her.' I looked at Suze again. 'What did you say to Nicola about the trip?'

'I told her that under the circumstances we couldn't possibly allow her to go on our behalf.' She glanced down at her hands and addressed her thumb nails. 'I also suggested that her resignation would be gratefully received.'

The sigh infected Rita next, then went around the table. We were all silent for a moment.

'I could take over the IRA client if someone else gave me a hand,' Maggie said at last, 'but there's no way I can go to Belfast on Thursday.' She looked over at Suze. 'Could you go?'

Suze turned to me. 'Dee should go.'

It was if she'd snapped an elastic band against my bare skin. 'Me?' Those sinister figures wearing balaclavas and pointing armalites and dripping blood from vampire grins reawoke in my mind.

For the first time since she'd sat down she smiled. 'I know Wiltshire Lucy rubbished my theory about Annie, but as the saying goes, "She would, wouldn't she?" And hard as you find it to swallow, it at least gives you another excuse to go over there. None of the rest of us has that.'

'None of the rest of us has a clue what you're talking about,' Rita said.

'Sorry,' Suze said. 'The manslaughter defence for Gillian Shiraz. The way I read some of the evidence, there's an off-chance that the victim Annie Murphy might have had a connection with the IRA.'

The conversation with Vic that I'd managed to forget since leaving the park clicked on and began to replay in my mind. *Annie Murphy had disappeared the day the news of Gerard Ryan's arrest first broke. Two of the IRA members Ryan had named to the authorities were called Murphy.*

The chance wasn't 'off' at all.

I let out the breath I'd been holding; there was no way out of this.

Five

The ground three floors below is tilting and rolling the way it does when you stand up after a Whirling Teacup ride. I struggle against the downwards pull of it, the urge if not to jump, then at least to stop resisting jumping.

Suddenly from behind me comes a scraping sound at the door. My heartbeat lurches, but my mind manages to sort out what is happening: someone is trying the key but can't get it to work. More fiddling and clattering go on. I am torn now between the sound and the swirling ground, but the sound has already broken the pull. I lean back into the room just as the door opens but am still too riveted by the moving middle distance to turn and look. Whoever's entered gasps, speaks an unintelligible curse, and strides towards me, high heels clacking on the hard floor. Hands take rough hold of my elbow and pull me all the way in. She slams the window and speaks again but again I can't quite distinguish the words.

I put my free hand on my chest, shake my head to indicate weakness, then lean on the bottom of the window frame for support. It's a bright morning – sunshine, cold blue sky – and while I'm staring out at it, I concentrate on bringing my rocking world to a stop. Gradually it steadies and, when it has, I realise I can make out now what was obscured by the night: the soldiers, for example, who as I'm watching pass in front of the corrugated metal fence across the road – three of them together moving forwards, one twenty yards behind walking backwards, all in riot gear, all with rifles out – I can see that they are British. The jeep that appears left and drives by, the helicopter that comes in towards me from the horizon and passes overhead – they are British too. The surviving wall of the derelict building that abuts the corrugated fence is covered by a mural showing a line of men, shoulder to shoulder, each in camouflage suit, balaclava and resistance beret, gun pointing at the onlooker. Beneath is the graffiti 'Vote Sinn Fein'.

I want to know what I'm doing *here* but am still formulating the question when the woman tugs at my arm. I turn and am instantly diverted by the familiarity of the eyes looking into mine. I don't recognise the rest of the oval face – the cropped auburn hair, the full mouth, the mole (oddly glamorous) just wide of the top lip – only that bridge across the nose . . .

She is young but irritation adds age to her expression. She points at the bed and speaks again. This time I know the words have to mean 'get back in there' but am disconcerted by the inability of my ear to cut through the accent to the message.

'What?' I say. It's a dumb sound.

'Lie down,' she enunciates. She redoubles the emphasis of the pointing finger. 'You shouldn't be standing up. You should be in bed. The drug's not worn off.' She's trying to be fierce with me but the lilt of her delivery ends in an upbeat that undermines her effort. She sighs as if she knows this too well.

A dog appears in the doorway, a mongrel with hound ears and an old spaniel's eyes. Behind it appear a boy, then a girl, then another boy, all under ten, all with hands over mouths, up to something they know perfectly well to be wicked. She turns on them sharply with the same pointed finger and they freeze where they are. 'Ay,' she says, 'go on with you now. *Out!*' They pretend to obey but actually just duck back a step. They're all dark-haired and two wear light-blue plastic National Health spectacles with thick lenses and I know without even knowing I know that they are not hers. Anyway she's much too young (surely) to have children that size.

She turns back to me, hands on her hips.

My tongue is still heavier than it should be but I say, 'Who are you? What am I doing here?'

She says, 'Excuse me, *I'm* the one who should be asking questions.'

I'm searching for the energy to argue this with her, when the wail of the baby rises through the floor. The woman implores the ceiling with her eyes, clicks her tongue, again points emphatically to the bed. 'I'll be back,' she promises over her shoulder.

I mutter 'I should hope so too,' but my fierceness is as ineffectual as hers and I don't think she even hears me.

Dog and children are shooed into the hall and the door is banged shut behind them. There is no sound of key in lock, just the sound of a tumble of footfall heading down the stairs. I wait until my heartbeat quietens, then move on tiptoe to the door. I press my ear against it but hear nothing closer than the noises from below. I glance at the bed: I could just get back into it. I don't need to do this.

I take a long inbreath, fill lungs and diaphragm right up, then reach for the knob, which I begin to turn and continue turning, ever so infinitesimally, until the latch makes a mute click; then I begin to inch it open, cringing at the creaking it makes. Two inches, three, four, six, a foot. I let out some breath and then, suddenly, a bespectacled face peers around the edge of the door and stares up at me, eyes hugely wide with magnification. I am so startled I gasp and step back but don't let go of the door knob and the door comes with my hand and gives me a knock on the forehead. It isn't that hard, in fact, but it's enough to start the room whirling again. I lose my balance and sit down heavily. How long must I put up with this confusion, I wonder, *how long?*

Then, abruptly, it lifts.

I

I woke up abruptly in the middle of the night thinking: if Annie Murphy was the person she seemed from Suze's speculations and Vic's findings – if she was some kind of Irish terrorist who'd got involved with the peace camp as a means of getting into the American missile base – if she wasn't the woman Gillian believed she was and Wiltshire Lucy believed she was and even I, come to that, believed she was – then what was I doing pursuing this angle? I didn't *need* to find her killer in order to prove it *wasn't*

Gillian Shiraz. With enough of the right technical evidence, it would be enough simply to prove the death occurred somewhere outside Annie's room and that, wherever that place was, Gillian couldn't possibly have been there. Thorny issues like who had sought to cover things up and let my client take the blame I could leave for the police to grasp.

I threw back the covers intending to get up and find my notebook but the instant I swung my legs over the side of the bed and sat upright the nausea rose in my stomach and I had to lie back down. As I was pulling the blanket back up to my chin I remembered my clinic appointment.

The clinic! I couldn't go to Belfast and miss *that*.

I thought about my duty to the alleged IRA terrorist bequeathed to the firm by Nicola's ambitions. I had glanced into her file after the meeting, just before I'd spoken to Theresa on the phone to tell her what had happened and say I'd be travelling with her to Belfast, but I recollected only the basics. Name: Maire Kelly. Age: 23. Place of birth: Derry. Occupation: Waitress. Place of arrest: Stockton-on-Tees. If I was honest about my feelings I had to admit that no matter how much I told myself she was just another client in need of legal representation to make sure she got a fair deal from the courts, the mere thought of getting involved with her filled me with dread.

Why are you torturing yourself Dee?

I decided on an approach and as soon as I got into the office rang Theresa again. 'Look,' I started, 'about this trip tomorrow . . .'

'Oh – good – glad you've phoned. I was going to ring you after lunch. Shall we meet at Heathrow?'

'Listen,' I asserted across her, 'I don't think . . .'

But her verbal momentum was blocking her ears. '. . . British Airways counter. Check-in's an hour and a half before take off and you *have* to be there that early to get through the security . . .'

'Theresa,' I insisted, '*listen* to me. I don't think I'll be able to go.'

That got through. 'Not be able to? But you *have* to, surely? What about Maire?' Her voice rose with surprise at me.

'I – ah – yes. But I wondered – there are only a couple of her relatives whose statements are crucial and I forgot all about this doctor's appointment, you see, which I'd rather not postpone if I can possibly help it. I wondered if you might . . .'

'Doctor's appointment? Is something wrong, Dee?'

'No, or rather what I mean is, I – I'm – well, I'm . . .' But there, abruptly, the words died. I couldn't tell her about that – not over the phone like this, baldly and as an excuse. And what could I possibly make up? Anything I'd make up was bound to sound feeble or get me into some ridiculous long-term lie.

I had only just realised this when I heard myself confess out loud to her a truth I'd not even admitted quietly inside my own mind. 'Actually, Theresa,' I told her, 'I'm frightened. I understand the issues and I can imagine how terrible it must be for the Catholics in west Belfast, but the violence of the place . . .'

But her laugh cut me off there, enveloping my ear in fondness. 'Oh Dee,' she said, 'I *am* sorry. I completely forgot that you've never been to the North.'

'Yes, well,' I rushed in defensively, 'so maybe I have misconceptions. The point is . . .'

'The point is now you're getting the chance to correct them – and in *excellent* company.' Her effort to jolly me was clear even if it didn't work. 'I won't let anything happen to you, I promise. We'll go around together to each . . . oops – hang on . . .' She put her hand over the mouthpiece and I heard muffled mutterings, quite heated, from her side. Finally, though, she came back. 'Sorry Dee, it's all go here today. Look, don't worry, everything will be fine, OK? I'll see you at the airport . . . no – tell you what, I'll come by for you. Six o'clock. Be ready.'

I put myself to sleep that night counting the injustices of the way the British government ruled Northern Ireland but dreamed of dark-hooded figures in blood-stained camouflage uniforms pointing rifles at me.

Nerve got me up and dressed: I could feel it whirring around in my gut like the cat who can't let go of its own tail. Then it pulled me along through all those steps I never thought I'd be able to manage: coming on to Theresa as if I were perfectly all right – 'normal' again – after my little flutter the day before, chatting with her on the way to the airport about this and that (but not 'it'), checking in. I even steadied myself against the hostility I expected from the security officers, who would be bound, Theresa had warned me, to look on us as enemies simply because they looked on our clients that way.

In the event the experience was more odd than threatening. While I was answering truthfully that I could not tell the Special Branch officer questioning me who I would be staying with because I did not know, and assuring her of my intention to return within forty-eight hours, the reality of it kept waving at me over her shoulder: here we were, going not to a foreign country, as it felt, but to another part of the UK. We would be there in less time than it took me to get from my flat to my office on the bus on a trafficky day; in less time than it took to fly from New York to Boston.

Imagine, I thought: what if the FBI could stop you before you boarded the Boston shuttle at LaGuardia – ask you a lot of personal questions – turn you back when they found something suspect in your ideological baggage?

. . . Would Scotland be next? Wales?

It was a clear morning and, as we boarded, a notice predicted a journey time of less than an hour. I stopped at our row, slid across to the window seat, dropped myself down, inhaled till I was full of breath; let it out on a long sigh.

Theresa took the seat beside me. 'Feeling OK?' she asked.

'Fine,' I said. Then I thought, why am I being so cagey with her? Was it embarrassment? Shame? Or simply sense of privacy?

Be brave. Unload.

I cleared my throat. 'You know that – "operation" – you had back when you worked for us?'

Unfortunately it was a bit too forthright. She flinched and averted her face as if I'd slapped it, then recovered by fishing into her bag.

'Oh God I'm sorry,' I said. 'I didn't meant to . . .'

She cut me off with a wave of her hand. 'I'm feeling guilty about it again, that's all. Brian and I – we've been trying to have a kid for the past eighteen months.'

'Theresa, I had no idea . . .'

'No, well, I haven't wanted to say anything to anyone – superstition I suppose. Anyway, we've both just been for tests and it looks like it's me – I've got some blockage.' She shook her head. 'If I'd ever thought it was going to be my only chance . . .'

I didn't know what to say so I reached over and gripped her on the forearm. 'Maybe . . .'

But she waved her hand: she wanted to change the subject. 'Did I tell you the plan for when we arrive?'

I let go and sat back. 'Nope.'

'OK, well, I'm now acting for *three* of the people they say Gerard Ryan named to the authorities, two in the same family, and all the relatives and friends I need to see live in west Belfast. Your client Maire's people live there too, so I've arranged for us to start at Divis Flats and move out, which means we end up doing one of mine, one of yours, one of mine today and the rest tomorrow. What I don't know is when we'll fit in interviews for this other case you mentioned. What's it about again?'

'Manslaughter. They want it to be Revenge of the Jealous Lesbian Lover but it's possible the victim had some kind of link with your ex-client.'

'With Gerard Ryan? Really? In that case some leads could easily emerge for you while we're talking to the people we have appoinments with.' She pointed down towards the briefcase under her seat. 'I've brought my clippings file on him – help yourself.'

'I've seen clippings. Vic gave me a wodge.'

'Did he? Where from?'

'The usual – national press, major locals, a few magazines.'

'English? Scots? Irish?'

I had to think about that a moment. 'Just English.'

This time she was the one who took the big inbreath and let out the long sigh. 'Listen . . .' she started. But suddenly the seat belt and no smoking signs came on and we became distracted by the rituals of take-off. After we were airborne, though, and after we'd watched a moment while the cabin crew began their assault on the previous London to Belfast record for distributing and collecting little plastic breakfast trays, Theresa said, 'Show me what you have, will you?'

I retrieved my case, got out the file, opened it and pulled out the clipping on top, a half-page article from one of the quality papers. A grainy black and white photograph of Ryan was reproduced in the middle of it and what it showed me was a shadowy, sinister man, glaring at the camera with hard eyes; his too-long hair was stringy, his face unshaven, and one side of his upper lip was curled (or so *I* thought) by a sneer. Such a face, I could believe, would hide itself under one of those death's-head hoods. Such a face would commit mindless atrocities against innocents.

Theresa looked across my shoulder at the piece and shook her head. I took this for distaste and expressed my own by pointing to one instance, then another, then the next in the catalogue of violent attacks he was reputed to have orchestrated: a pub bombing, a cabinet minister's assassination, the deaths of army bandsmen during a concert. The journalist who'd written it was eloquent in his suppressed outrage and his unmentioned horror peaked in his descriptions of the wounds of the victims and survivors. Ryan was a madman, that's all one could conclude. Just a madman.

Theresa was still shaking her head. 'But what does this tell us about *him*?' she said. 'Look – it tells us *nothing*.'

Quite honestly I hadn't picked that up, but now that she'd pointed it out I saw she was right. 'Mmmm,' I said, 'yes – now that you mention it the only personal detail I can remember from any of those clips is his age: he's in his mid-forties. It stuck because I thought he sounded on the old side for an activist... That may have been how he survived so long – the knack for keeping a low profile.'

'You mean you reckon they don't know any more about him than they print?'

I shrugged. That, I realised, was what I must have been assuming – not that I'd really thought about it.

She lifted her case to her lap, unpopped the catches, took out a folder, went through it, sorted out a handful of clippings. She then selected one of these and laid it out on the lid of her case. This was also half a page and the photo in the middle of it was of a man I didn't recognise. The print quality wasn't much better than in my clipping but this face was relaxed, these eyes amused, this hair neat, this lip turned up by a smile.

'Who's this?'

'Gerard Ryan.'

I waved my clipping at her. 'You mean this isn't him?'

'No,' she said. She tapped the picture of him in her clipping. 'I mean *this* is what he really looks like – that picture you've got there was released by Special Branch. It was taken at the end of the seven days he spent in custody "helping with enquiries" before I was allowed in to see him.'

She turned it over – it had been cut from an Irish paper – turned it back and handed it to me. 'He is not actually a psychopathic killer who came from nowhere to wreak carnage on the innocent. That's government propaganda; a tabloid fiction.'

I took the clipping from her. I knew about propaganda and tabloid fiction – I didn't as a rule need to be persuaded – but I was puzzled to hear her using these terms about Ryan. 'I don't understand, Theresa. Are you defending the guy? The last time we talked about him you'd just worked out that he must have shopped his comrades to MI5 and could find no words for his treachery.'

'Yes, I know . . .'

'. . . And it was your anger – I mean, if you hadn't felt so disgusted I probably wouldn't have asked you about tipping Vic the story.'

She nodded, not disputing this version of events. 'Yes – well – that was *before*.' She lurched forward suddenly and peeked over the top of the seats in front of us; then, rolling her eyes at me as if to say 'whew', she slouched back in her seat, leaned her head closer to mine and turned her voice down to a mere underbreath. '. . . *before* I heard about the conspiracy theory that's been doing the rounds in west Belfast the past week or so.'

In a burst of instinct I knew how the new theory went. 'Don't tell me,' I said. 'They're saying he's been framed to look like a grass and we've all been manipulated – lawyers, press, public, the lot. . . . Am I close?'

She was nodding again. 'And if it's true – which I can believe – we should be ashamed of ourselves. We've been led into biting on *the* most circumstantial of evidence: he sacks me, he's moved from

Brixton Prison, alleged IRA members in England are rounded up, and we jump to the conclusion we're meant to jump to. Not only that, we use a security services "mole" to confirm it.... In this way have two left-wing lawyers and a left-wing journalist been used to spread disinformation.'

'You really believe that?'

'It's not a question of "belief", it's a question of the evidence, and the more I think about what there is on Gerard Ryan and his life to this point, the more it adds up to a picture of the last man on earth who'd turn informer... even if they beat him to *death*. He had nothing whatsoever to gain, not one single thing.'

'Whereas they . . . ?'

'... Whereas *they*, as usual, gain publicity points: yes friends, here it is, another great victory in the war against terrorism. Even more deviously, though, they neutralise their prisoner; he doesn't need to say a single word in court. Just the fact that he was supposed to have named names means he'll never be completely trusted – by anyone.'

I leaned back against the head rest and stared into the molecular motions of the air just beyond the tip of my nose. It wasn't inconceivable: judging by the kiss and tell revelations of former spies, what the security services really got up to was even more arcane than the fictions about it. On the other hand, Theresa's opinion could hardly be described as non-partisan. Wasn't she bound to be attracted to any theory that justified her position?

Perceiving my scepticism, she thrust at me the rest of the clippings she'd picked out of her collection. 'Read,' she said.

I read – and at first became quite excited. Here at last, I thought: the inner workings of an alleged terrorist. As I continued reading, though, I began to discern a new bias. According to this Gerald Ryan was but the latest offshoot of a noble warrior line. Its most legendary figure has been his grandfather, Liam; he'd gone to prison rather than serve in the British Army in the early days of the First World War; he'd 'stood shoulder to shoulder with Connolly' in Dublin during the 1916 Easter Rising and fought in the civil war; he'd moved to Belfast to help continue 'the struggle' in the six Northern counties that the new Irish Free State didn't get from Britain; he'd been interned by the British in the late fifties; he'd even died in prison.

Gerard's father Joseph had inherited these heroic tendencies. He was arrested on suspicion of various explosives charges several times before he was twenty. When Britain began to talk about conscripting Catholics from the North to fight against Hitler, he was part of the movement that made them drop the idea. He was interned in the early sixties and spent time in the same cell where his father had died.

Other Ryans – great-uncles, uncles, cousins – had committed equally valorous deeds, but military history, I'm afraid, always tends to lose me, and this small chapter was no exception.

I glanced at Theresa, who was reading a book, then stared out the window a moment at the little puffs of white cloud. I would just look at one more clipping – I was nearly to the bottom of the pile – then maybe doze. My eyes began to skim – it wasn't actually a bad piece, the first part of a three-part profile – my lids got heavier, I blinked myself to. Then, unexpectedly, I made a discovery: Gerard Ryan as a young man had been as unimpressed by his warrior forebears as I was. In fact, he'd been *so* unimpressed he'd refused to follow his elders into the Republican movement. Instead he'd gone out and found himself a part in a fairy tale.

He was the prince charming, that's how it seemed – a lad of eighteen just starting work as an apprentice electrician. The princess was a sixteen-year-old girl with blonde hair, dimples and green eyes who according to both sets of parents was much too young. They married anyway as soon as they could and showed everyone up by becoming best friends and genuinely enjoying the children that came one after the other their first four years. When the miracle happened and they actually got a small house of their own off the council in about 1965, it was widely agreed that there were no two ways about it, the young couple were destined to a life of happy ever after.

That it didn't quite pan out that way was because of the location of the small house, which was in the then mixed Rathcode neighbourhood. The Ryans liked the fact that their kids sat beside Protestant kids at school and that birthday parties were excuses for families to have meals at each other's houses; and because they were so content they ignored the civil rights movement when it started in the late sixties. They also ignored it when relatives muttered about 'Uncle Toms'. They ignored the violence at first, too – ignored the firebombings mere blocks away, ignored the implications when one close Catholic friend, then another, then a third and a fourth lost homes or cars or pets. It was only when lives began to be lost that the ignoring began to crack and Gerard let himself be dragged off to one or two meetings. He was still dithering about what to do: to emigrate to Canada? to move back over to the family neighbourhood again? to accept the message of his background? – when his fairy tale was touched by the wand of the wicked witch.

It happened not long before Christmas – early December 1969 at 4.30 p.m. on a black evening. His three older children were at a friend's; he was still at work, and his wife Mary was in the kitchen with her youngest daughter, making her a lemon drink for her cold, when suddenly there was a whistling noise through the air and a loud bang – all the neighbours heard it. It landed in the kitchen, went right through the roof and through the ceiling and exploded (they said) at the feet of the two people he loved most in the world.

This, said the journalist author of the profile, was when Gerard Ryan first offered to work for the IRA.

II

It had never crossed my mind to consult a guide book about Belfast. I'd seen enough pictures on TV. I knew what a great ugly smouldering heap of a place it was. So when the coach driving us in from the airport reached the crest of a long slow incline and it was suddenly there in the distance, I wasn't at all prepared – not for a range of winter green hills, dramatic against back-lit black clouds, with bits of city poking out of its pockets. It made me wish I'd brought along a pad and watercolours.

The centre, when we finally got into it, was equally unexpected. A cross between London after the blitz, in the sepia and white tones of the Pathé cinema news reports, and Beirut in the second half of the eighties – that's what I'd imagined . . . Oh yes and modest, on the scale of a shabby overgrown town. Instead it was grand in that neo-classical manner you find in Liverpool and Glasgow and the other *urbs* the Victorians erected in the pink of their industrial prosperity.

'It's also the exclusive preserve of the Protestant upper middle class,' Theresa said out of the corner of her mouth at me as we got off the coach. 'Where we're headed now on the other hand . . . Oh! Look!' She jabbed her finger at the air towards a black London taxi approaching from the left, waved at me to hurry and set out towards it at a run.

I knew of course about the black taxis of Belfast – I may have forgotten I knew, but I knew. I'd seen a documentary years before that had gone into the whole story: how the official bus service had stopped running into the Catholic areas in the early seventies, how local drivers had set up a co-op to replace it, how they'd imported a load of reconditioned black cabs to use as minibuses. It was still disconcerting, though, when I saw that first one pull in to the kerb and heard the characteristic knock of its diesel engine as it idled.

Divis Flats were pretty disconcerting too, and this despite the fact that I'd seen them in the background of countless news clips and had arrived expecting ugliness. What I wasn't at all ready for – hadn't begun to comprehend – was the extent of that ugliness: block after concrete block, plugged like so many six-storey multipoint sockets into the rubble between the nineteen-storey tower to one side and the twin spires of a Gothic church to the other. Add a mesh fence topped with razor wire and some armed guards and, abracadabra biddidy bob, a prison – so it seemed to me and so I muttered to Theresa after the taxi let us off.

She gestured upward with her head and eyes. I followed with mine and saw that the top floor windows of the tower were blacked out. I frowned, not understanding.

'Army,' she said. 'They watch everything that goes on here –' She put her mouth to my ear and spoke the rest in a Belfast accent: '– through the sights of their wee guns.'

I suddenly wished to hell I'd worn a wide-brimmed hat and dark glasses and began to look around a little wildly for cover.

When I saw there wasn't any, I turned and headed into this unlikely looking sanctuary.

Closer in I realised what was wrong with the impressions left by the TV news: the cameras were both too close and too far away. They couldn't encompass the far moonscape quality of the terrain but also missed the rusting coloured panels that must have looked so neat ('design-wise') twenty years ago on some architect's drawing board; nor had they showed me that the graffiti came in layers, today's angry slogan spray-painted over yesterday's. The camera's biggest deceit, though, arose from its lack of a nose: it couldn't record, never mind pass on, the stench of backed-up drains, of alcoholic piss fermenting under the covered walkways, of rubbish turning to compost on the unlit stairwells.

We laboured up to the fifth floor of the third or fourth block we came to, a block with so many windows blindfolded by hoarding that I didn't at first see how anyone could possibly be living there. Theresa led us confidently, however, into a right-turn on the landing, then stopped in front of the door of the first unit we came to that was still occupied.

As she set down her case and her sleeping bag, she said, more to herself than to me, 'I hope her mother's been able to get here.' 'Her' was one of Theresa's clients and this was the flat where her sister lived.

'What would keep her away?'

She began unpeeling her right glove. 'She was hit by a plastic bullet last year.' She put her newly exposed fingers to her eyes. 'Here.'

I winced. I dread loss of sight almost more than anything.

She shrugged as if to say 'how could you expect anything else?', then turned to the door. She tapped out a little rhythm on it that might have been a code and a moment later there were shouts, the over-excited commanding ones of small boys, followed by stampeding feet. Next there was a collision of bodies on the other side of the door, a scrabbling noise against it, and finally, an opening. Half a dozen children, all slightly too young for school, stood across the entrance, jostling with each other to get a look at us. Behind them a blonde woman emerged and, smiling a wide glad-to-see-you smile, waved at Theresa.

Theresa laughed and waved back.

The woman clapped her hands together as if shooing pigeons, plucked a toddler from the floor, propped it on her hip, and said something I didn't catch. The rest of the children were suddenly not there, however, and we passed through. A second woman appeared, our coats were removed from us, introductions were made, initial chatter started up, and my comprehension remained minimal: chewed-hard 'r's and an upbeat, that was about as far as I got. I could read gestures, though, especially the one meaning come into the warm and have a cup of tea, and I pushed open the door that was obviously *the* door. The small room seemed crowded out with women, though there were in fact only four, all of whom stood when I entered and welcomed me with the same degree of pleasure the blonde woman had shown – or rather all of them stood but one. She simply smiled and extended her long frail fingers in greeting. She wore glasses with black lenses in them and a walking stick was propped against the side of her armchair.

A cup of tea found its way into one of my hands, a chocolate digestive into the other. Several different conversations started up, all about Theresa's client and how she was and what her chances were, and I moved my ear around between them, trying to get it tuned in. It was an effort though, especially in such a stuffy smoky room, and my attention kept wandering – now around the decor: the peeling ceiling paper, the fungus on the walls, the condensation on the window panes that was a sign of poor ventilation – now to the rubbery sense of tiredness in my limbs that I could have done without.

I excused myself and made my way out into the hall again but did not find much respite in the small bathroom, where the walls were so wet they were spongy and there was a heavy smell of mildew. The face looking back at me in the streaky mirror was uncharacteristically gaunt, with no colour in its cheeks at all.

A round of musical chairs had been played out while I'd been away and the empty one I took up gave me a sideways profile view of the blind woman, whose scarred sockets were right in my sight line. My imagination began to produce images of what it must have been like for her: the sound of the shot; the impact of the high velocity cylinder smashing the bones of the face; the blacking out; the coming to and finding everything still black.

I pulled my gaze away – it was time to forsake the periphery – and retrieving my bag, signalled to Theresa, who managed to orchestrate a lull. I held up the more recent of the two prints I'd brought with me, and feeling terribly conscious of my American accent and middle-class professional manners, said: 'The death of this woman, Anne Murphy – Annie as I knew her – may be linked either to Gerard Ryan's arrest or to his disclosures to the authorities. The suggestion I'm here trying to follow up is that she may have been involved with an IRA cell in England.'

The faces looking at me each seemed to adjust ever so slightly – the smiles, the interest in what I was saying, the warmth, were still there, only now they were coming from several feet further back.

The photo was taken from my hand and started on its rounds among the women.

I held up the other one. 'This is her as a girl, with her mother. The parents were presumably killed in the same fire that left her badly scarred. She was looked after by foster parents named Christine and Joseph Murphy – they used to live outside Glasgow and seem to have been relatives. If anybody can put me in touch with either of them . . .'

This photo too was now plucked from me and began to circulate. Heads were bent over in scrutiny, making expressions impossible to read, but when the first photo reached the third woman, she leaned sideways towards the woman who'd given it to her. Murmurings impossible to make out went back and forth between them. Then they separated and leaned towards the women to their other sides; more unintelligible mumblings went on.

Finally the woman who was now holding both the photos handed them back to me. 'Sorry,' she said. 'Can't help you.'

This time I had no problem with comprehension: 'can't' meant 'won't'.

Maire Kelly, the client I'd inherited from the departed Nicola, had a young aunt who lived on the top floor of the next block along, and she too had assembled a roomful of women for us to talk to – two were Maire's cousins, two more had gone to school with her, one had taught her there. This time as I accepted a mug of tea and passed along the plate of chocolate biscuits, I realised what must have been sacrificed for such an act of hospitality. This was a woman, after all, who was supporting three children on supplementary benefit while her husband was in gaol.

Not that she seemed to feel any bitterness or shame or frustration; on the contrary. 'My Seamus,' she said to me, 'is not some kind of common criminal. The British Army is a foreign army of occupation and he was fighting against it. He's a political prisoner.' She was equally proud of her father, her elder brother, her father-in-law and her husband's younger brother, all of whom had also served time for the same reason – and now her niece Maire, too, the first woman in the family to be put behind bars.

I took a lot of notes and when I surfaced from my pad and rejoined the conversation around Theresa, it had moved on to Gerard Ryan and the whys and wherefores of his treachery – *if* it was treachery. One of Maire's school friends was saying, 'I don't believe them that says he didn't do it.'

A cousin said, 'But it's a perfect set-up.'

'If it's that then why have they let his Shivawn out of prison?'

There was complete silence for a full moment; then Maire's aunt said, 'When did that happen?'

'Yesterday. Two days before the wain was due to be taken away from her.' She looked at me. 'It's Gerard Ryan's only grandchild.'

I filtered a short suck of air between my teeth: there it was – his motive, the insoluble mystery solved. 'Have they been taken into protective custody?'

The speaker shook her head. 'Shivawn refused it. That's why she wasn't let go when he first done it – so's I've heard.'

As we headed west up the Falls Road in another black cab I searched the ordinary working class areas and council estates we passed for the smouldering heap images I'd brought with me, but here again saw no sign of them – or didn't until we came within sight of a police station. Suddenly, there they all were: front doors muzzled with wire cages, nearby sites bandaged with corrugated hoarding, barbed-wire barricades, armoured vehicles, even foot patrols in spaceman riot helmets with bullet packs strapped on like prosthetic breasts, rifles ready. Overhead – louder and louder as it approached, more and more muffled as it went back – came the clatter of the blades of a helicopter carving an elliptical surveillance pattern above us.

Neither Theresa nor the other passengers in the taxi nor any of the people on the pavement seemed to notice any of it.

We arrived eventually at Andersonstown, a sprawling suburb that, if my name were Anderson, I would take more as an insult than a testament to immortality. Here we were welcomed into a third household with more of the same enthusiastic hospitality which again lasted throughout discussions of their relative and the factors for and against Gerard Ryan's guilt, only to freeze when I took out the photos of Annie Murphy. I began to suspect there was a message here and when it happened at the end of the next interview too, I said to Theresa, 'Look, I must be warm about something. I can feel everyone seize up when I get to it. I've got to find out if I'm in a cul-de-sac or just a blocked tunnel and this is too long a way to be going about it. I want to go to the Records Office – look up Ryan's family – see if I can find a link to Annie's foster parents.'

One of her eyebrows arched. I knew it was a long shot though, did not need her to remind me, so ignored the look (ignored, indeed, the weariness in my limbs and the tightness in my stomach), and checked my watch. 'It's almost 1.30,' I persisted. 'I don't need to stop for lunch. A sandwich will do me.'

The eyebrow had resettled and she shrugged like 'what the hell'. 'Fine by me,' she said, 'I've got one or two things I can check out in the newspaper archives.'

After a call to say we were rejigging the itinerary, we picked up a third taxi and re-wound our way east to the grandiose city centre. I don't know what I expected at the Records Office – questions about our business? a thorough search of our handbags? certainly *some* kind of bureaucratic confrontation – but the guard waved us in after a brief glance in our bags.

I started with the microfiche marriage records, which were in alphabetical order within date groupings, and established without too much trouble that the maiden name of Gerard Ryan's late wife Mary had been O'Neill. I searched out the files of her parents, then followed a course through the birth records, but among all the grandmothers and sisters and sisters-in-law and aunts and cousins there wasn't a sign of the Christine who, as the wife of a Joseph Murphy, had been Annie's foster mother.

I decided while I was at it to look up Mary Ryan's death certificate too, to confirm the cause and to find out the exact date when she and her daughter had been killed by the Loyalist firebomb. Once I had this information, I could go into the news archives, read up on the incident and look out for a Christine in the reports. For some reason, though, I couldn't seem to find it.

I can get like that sometimes – can't see what's in front of me – so I made a note to go back to it and moved on to Ryan, Gerard Patrick, born Belfast 1940, and his parents, beginning with his mother. When that produced nothing, I tried his two sons, neither of whom turned out to be married, his brothers, his sisters, his brothers' wives, his brothers' wives sisters; I then looked up his daughter Shivawn, whose name it turned out was spelled 'Siobhan', a word which in my head I'd always pronounced 'See-ob-han'. Finally, just to make sure I'd covered everything, I looked up the daughter who'd been killed. What I discovered here was that I couldn't locate the death certificate for her either.

I sat back in the straightbacked chair and considered this for a moment, but my thoughts began to multiply and crescendo so fast I had to abandon them. I sat forwards once more and went back to the microfiche, back to Mary Ryan, and looked again. This time when I couldn't find her death certificate I scrolled up and down to see if the information was maybe misfiled.

I found no evidence of this.

I had another look for the daughter.

– More nothing –

I went to find the librarian and brought him back to my table, where I explained the problem.

He frowned and bent over the machine. 'Mmmm,' he murmured as he looked at the screen, 'complete death certificate data *is* on record here.' Then he went through the same process of checking and double-checking I'd gone through, to exactly the same effect.

Frowning more deeply, he stood up to height again and looked at me. 'You're certain there *was* a death?'

I got out the article Theresa had given me on the plane and showed it to him. 'The journalist interviewed the husband and father. I wouldn't have thought you could get more certain than that.'

He read and when he finished, nodded. 'I'll check the old index card file. Once in a while we do find that a piece of pre-1975 data hasn't been correctly transferred.' And he disappeared.

I got out the newspaper I'd brought with me, finding it odd now to read morning headlines from what seemed another dimension, and had only just skimmed the law reports when he returned.

'I'm sorry,' he said without sounding at all sorry, 'but these deaths could not possibly have taken place in this area.'

'Do you cover all of Belfast? Maybe I'm in the wrong office.'

'There isn't any other.'

'Then your records must be incomplete.'

He shook his head. 'Impossible. If it happened it will be here.'

Irritated by his unyielding confidence (so typically male) and pretty well finished anyway, I thanked him tersely, picked up my coat, and went to see how Theresa was getting on. She was nearly done – would be only a moment more – and I, feeling still riled without being clear quite why, went outside to stand on the front steps of the building to wait for her in the crisp air of the lowering twilight.

I had been standing there, I don't know, a good three or four minutes – was so frozen I was hopping from foot to foot to keep warm – was contemplating a return to the indoors – had stopped thinking about the case and my failure to progress it, never mind about the librarian – when suddenly I caught an echo of what he'd said as it passed across the back of my mind.

'If it happened it will be here.'

I hurried inside to get Theresa.

What I had to do was clear enough: I had to talk to Siobhan Ryan.

'Get in the queue,' Theresa laughed when I told her.

After our morning's conversations, however, I was quite aware that when a woman's liberty is said to be the intelligence services' reward to her father for naming names, *everybody* wants to talk to her. It didn't matter though; couldn't matter; I had to try.

I said, 'I think the best thing to do is stop in on everyone again on the way back – tell them all straight out that I want to arrange a meeting with Siobhan – ask them to put it around their grapevines.'

Theresa too became serious. 'Not necessary,' she said. 'There's a shortcut: there's a woman at the Sinn Fein office I want to make an appointment with to talk about these bloody exclusion orders.' Of the dozen or so people we'd interviewed, about two thirds were invariably stopped, detained for questioning and turned away if they tried to enter Scotland, Wales or England. This included the three so far who were prepared to stand up in a British court and testify on behalf of one or another of our clients. 'If there's one person in a position to spread the word, it's her.' She took a look at her watch and shrugged. '*If* she's in.'

We returned by taxi into the Catholic section, up the Falls Road, and were headed for Andersonstown again when Theresa tapped on the glass and the driver pulled to the kerb. It had started to rain and wet rubbish glistened under the dim light of a solitary still-functioning street lamp. There was little traffic, just the occasional car passing the occasional armoured vehicle. Pulling our coats up over our heads, we ran along the pavement, me behind Theresa, until she stopped at the ramshackle gate of what looked to me like a derelict house.

This was headquarters of the group whose name the English media always referred to as 'Shin-Fane-the-political-wing-of-the-IRA'? How came such an empire of fiends to occupy such an impoverished dwelling?

'*This?*' I said, needing to hear her confirm it.

She answered by walking on through and along the path, up the steps to the door, on which she gave a couple of good firm knocks. When a guy answered, arms across his chest and feet on either edge of the threshold, she dusted off some Irish I hadn't known she had which caused him to stand aside as if she'd uttered the magic sesame.

Inside matched out for dank and decay, with funds apparently not even stretching across the difference between a 40- and a 60-watt bulb. We were guided in, first to a waiting room that owed a lot to the unlicensed betting rooms of the American thirties as depicted by Hollywood, and after we'd served our time there, up a narrow rickety flight of stairs to a small office at the top.

The woman who rose to us might have been fronting a City brokerage firm the way she extended a slender hand, smiled coolly and flicked back a drape of hair the colour and texture of grey fox. There was to be no small talk – it was the end of her long day too – and we'd barely sat down before Theresa had said what she'd come to say and the two of them had fixed up a time to get together the following afternoon. Suddenly it was my turn.

'Siobhan Ryan –' I started.

She gave me a look that said I might as well hold it right there, but doubling my speed instead, I gave her an abridged version of the story of Annie Murphy, her death and its circumstances. 'An innocent woman – a friend of Annie's who was staying in her flat – has been charged,' I rushed on. 'I've been trying to find out the truth and indications are now – well –' – and here for some reason I faltered and heard myself veer towards euphemism: '– indications are growing that the dead woman may have had a – ah – "connection" to Gerard Ryan. I need first-hand evidence and as his two sons are still, I understand, in prison, that leaves only one person who can give it to me.' Then I held out the old photo that I'd shown everyone else. 'This is Annie – Anne Marie – when she was about five, with her mother. A year or so later, in about 1970 or '71, she was badly burned all over her torso and her parents may have been killed; in any case Annie ended up at a convent outside Dumfries.'

The woman took the print from me and stared into it quite a long time – so long you knew she wasn't seeing *it* any more but had drifted away. Finally she blinked and dropped it on the desk, as if its weight or maybe its smell had just hit her. She slid it towards me with her fingertips. 'I don't know where Siobhan

Ryan is,' she said. Her tone was carefully matter-of-fact. 'And even if I did . . .'

I caught her eye and, holding it, leaned towards her. 'I'm not asking for her address. I simply want her to get in touch with me.'

She broke the contact, shifting her focus to the floor.

Theresa said, 'We'll be at Patrick Mahoney's place tonight and tomorrow night.'

The woman nodded. She had heard – she would keep what we'd said in mind – she made no promises. Then she stood up again: we were dismissed.

Outside once more, I found I'd run out of the nerve on which I'd been operating since we left the Records Office. I wanted now only to collapse in front of a television with a cup of something hot and let mind and body drain. I looked at Theresa. 'To the billet?'

She smiled that fond smile of hers and I realised what I'd done: I hadn't pronounced quotation marks around the word the way I had back in London when she'd first used it on me. Then it had struck me as a strangely macho term for the bed and breakfast accommodation her contact would be fixing up for us in a west Belfast home; in fact I'd quietly taken her need to evoke those long makeshift military barracks left over from World War Two as further evidence of her poetic view of the Irish. What I appreciated now was that she'd seen me seeing her that way but rather than correct me had bided her time.

Patrick's place turned out to be on the ground floor of a small block in a low-rise sixties public housing estate that, as far as I was concerned, was indistinguishable from the others we'd visited that day. Our host, a man of maybe forty-five in a freshly pressed workshirt and jeans, had two pokey rooms made pokier by his tolerance for clutter, which he only seemed to notice as we came in. As he moved a pile of clothes and books and cassette tapes and sheet music off the sofa on to the top of another similar pile on the armchair and bade us sit down, I realised the air was full of the smell of roasting chicken; I also realised how hungry I was.

More restacking of things went on, a cardtable appeared and was unfolded, a red paper tablecloth materialised, strong tea was poured into mugs. Over prawn cocktail, meat and two veg and trifle he probed us for details of our business in Belfast and, beginning with Theresa, from whom I took my lead, we told him. When I concluded my story by saying how badly I wanted to find Siobhan Ryan, he lifted cup to lips, sucked in the last droplet of cold tea, stood up and reached for his coat. 'There's only one place to go with that kind of problem,' he said. He waved at us to pick ourselves up then please and smartly. 'I was feeling a wee bit dry now anyway.'

I groaned and slumped back. Go out and drink? The way I was feeling? He had to be joking.

He let out a single bark, like a satisfied seal at feeding time. 'You Yanks – you're all just too mean to buy rounds.' His smile teased me. 'You keep your bloody fags to yourself too.'

There are times, I will confess now, when I can act as if deep down I believe that it's OK for *me* to criticise my fellow Americans but not for anybody else to do it (and certainly not a *foreigner*). This was one of those times.

I was on my feet immediately, hands gripping hips for emphasis. 'We have different customs,' I started, 'we're brought up to . . .' But suddenly my coat was being applied to my body and Theresa was somehow already out the door and nobody was listening.

The rain clouds had pulled back around a hole that was now filled with a nearly full moon and the temperature had dropped so much that the first few lungsful of air felt like icicles scratching across the capillaries. As we headed on foot towards the main road a couple of other people joined us, one of whom Theresa had met before, and when they got into conversation Patrick started telling me stories about other visitors he'd put up, from Palestine, Soweto, even from the Philippines. His favourites, though, were a couple from Mondragon. He cleared his throat and spoke a sentence in Spanish that meant approximately 'Which way to the men's ice cream?' Then he grinned. 'I'm going over to stay with them in the summer.'

I grinned back. 'You're not worried about being "excluded"?'

He looked at me like 'You can't be serious (*can* you?)' and I realised that I'd equated, quite unconsciously, British treatment of the Catholic people from the North of Ireland with European treatment of them. The truth, of course, was sadder and more ironic: here was a man, a British citizen, who would find it easier to pass into Spain or Italy or France than into Stranraer or Fishguard or Liverpool.

We turned up a drive on the other side of the main road, walked between some trees towards a whitewashed stucco public house, and let Patrick lead us through the front door. The bar was up a flight of stairs and when we got to it I made a big deal out of making sure he saw me buy the first round, then followed him and the others into a crowded lounge room. Everyone knew everyone, so there were lots of hellos and chats, and once we'd organised tables and chairs, got coats off and settled in, a guy who'd been strumming to himself on a guitar in the corner diagonally opposite strummed a louder chord, stood up, looked over at the woman Theresa had been talking to and said something to her in Irish. Everyone applauded and she laughed and walked over to join him. A flute player appeared, then a percussionist with a bodhran, and people began to call out requests. Suddenly it was two or three hours later, the top of the room was thick with used smoke, the table was covered with empty glasses, and my throat was hoarse from singing along. I hadn't yet, I realised, had a single conversation about Siobhan Ryan and what was more, my bladder was sending me emergency signals.

I knew my priorities and, judging my moment, lifted my body on to its rubbery legs and directed it carefully across the small room, through the people, towards the door out, whence I made my way back down the stairs to the ladies' room next to the entrance. The sense of nausea that came over me while I was standing in the queue I took for a late reminder that women in my condition are meant to stop drinking. When my turn came, however, I noticed two small spots of blood on my underpants and instantly thought, Whoopee! It's all been a false alarm! Then, just as quickly, I thought: or maybe . . .?

I decided it really was time to unburden myself to Theresa and, sobered by determination, let myself out of the cubicle. The place was empty now except for two other women, both using the sinks, and I made for the free one in between them. Concentrating hard, I manipulated the lump of soap and was rinsing off the result when hands gripped each of my elbows.

I opened my mouth to say 'hey'.

'Quiet' one hushed.

The other one crooked her index finger too close to the end of my nose. 'Come,' she said, 'this way.'

I went a few steps with her almost inadvertently but when I found myself being conducted to the exit, I baulked. 'My coat...'

Pressure was applied to the soft spots on either side of my elbow joints; I winced and my treacherous legs began to move again.

I was guided out into the now moonless darkness towards a group of parked cars. We wove through these into the middle where they stopped me beside the front passenger door of an old Volvo. As I stood there the window started to roll down, revealing a head with hair hidden under a knitted stocking hat and eyes masked by sun glasses; a scarf had been wound around the neck, partially concealing the mouth and chin. It could have been anybody, of any sex.

'Who are you?' asked a muffled female voice.

It could have been any female's, but I answered truthfully.

When I'd done this a gloved hand rose and flicked at me dismissively over the top of the window. 'Who are you *really*?'

'I just told you. I am really a lawyer from London. Look, if you're Siobhan Ryan, I just want to talk to you for a moment – I just need to ask you one question... In my bag there's a photo – I want to know – the girl in it...' But something was wrong: I felt unsteady. Had the women let go of my arms? What was going on? And then it came: the slash of pain that cut around from one side of my underbelly to the other.

I clutched myself and heard myself cry out, 'Don't – please – I'm pregnant.' Then I lost consciousness.

Six

A cup is pressing at my bottom lip and my mouth is filling with liquid. I spit it out and push the cup away.

'No more dope,' I say, '... enough.' I mean to sound fierce – fed up – but what comes out is feeble.

'This is just water. All I've given you is one pill,' – there is amusement at the corners of her mouth – 'and it's not worn off. That's why I told you to go back to bed.'

I am, I realise, sitting on the floor. She is squatting in front of me and gives off a faint smell of baby powder. I now seem able to understand every word she says. 'Why have you brought me here?' I try to demand in my pathetic voice. My memory is working well now, which makes this gap in it all the more alarming. 'What do you want with me?'

Her smile becomes laughter and her body starts to shake. In fact she's so entertained she throws back her head of dark auburn hair and lets off a couple of hoots at the ceiling. With this out of her system, she looks into my half-open blurry eyes with her amused, alert green ones (she is so young – not a line on her face) and says, 'You think I've kidnapped you – that's what it is, isn't it?'

If I hate anything it's being patronised, so I'm instantly stung into snapping back, 'I'm physically attacked, I'm drugged, I'm kept locked up in a room – is there another conclusion?'

She stands up and smooths her tight bleached jeans over her small thighs. Even in stiletto heels she's not much taller than I am, though maybe two thirds my size. As she changes position I notice that the girl with the glasses is bent over a baby on a blanket on the floor, trying to distract it with a stuffed rabbit no bigger than her hand. The boy is hanging back watching me through his thick lenses and the woman now gestures to him to wake up and come around to my other side. He obeys and she has him grip that arm while she grips the other and they begin to help me to my feet.

'The "physical attack",' she says, ignoring my efforts to push her hands away, 'came from your own body.' They get me up and steady enough on my legs to stand without support, and as she lets go of me she stares right into my eyes again. 'You drank too much. You fainted. I gave you a stematyl. You don't know stematyl? It's American. A friend's cousin sent it to her, and she gave it to me. It's for pregnant women – stops nausea and all that. Some women it knocks out – it knocked me out too, but it's harmless to the baby. You're here because we couldn't leave you in the car park – you might have miscarried. You still could. You must go back to bed.'

Inside me it's as though the cord has been yanked on venetian blinds, turning them all over. I step back from the stunning brightness.

I am here as a patient?

My God.

Then I remember the two small red blood spots on the cotton crotch of my underpants, the pain that cut under my belly before I passed out, and hear an echo of my voice crying out 'I'm pregnant'.

I had thought about me rejecting it but not about it rejecting me.

I return to bed at once and when I'm settled again under the blankets, she feeds me more water. I drink it all and as I hand her back the cup I begin to feel the energy returning to my arms and legs. I'm becoming me again.

'You're Siobhan Ryan,' I say.

In answer she makes a fist of her left hand and holds it out so I can see the gold band on the ring finger. '*Was.*' Then she points to the empty plate on the table. 'You hungry?'

I remember the smell of that burning toast and my stomach rolls over in its own juices, making a loud noise as it turns. I nod at once – am I *ever* – and out of nowhere recollect why I'd wanted to see her so desperately. I say, 'My handbag – I need . . .'

'It's downstairs. I'll bring it back with me. Your clothes are still in the sink I'm afraid.' She turns to the girl. 'Put Shona on here,' she pats the foot of the bed, 'and help the woman if she needs anything.' Then she taps the boy on the shoulder and leads him towards the door.

The girl introduces herself as Marie Louise, and leans on her elbows on the bed to watch the baby. She tells me how her uncle was shoved out of this room so Siobhan and her child could have it and how *they* were then shoved out of it so I could have it.

'Oh dear,' I say, sitting further upright so I can stroke the down on the baby's head. 'Where is everyone sleeping?'

It turns out there has been a highly complex series of shifts and reshuffles involving the living room floor, the sofa and the neighbour's son's sleeping bag, and she is only in the middle of describing what's gone on when there is a sudden outcry of misery. We have not been paying enough attention.

Marie Louise lifts the unhappy infant off the spread, drapes her across her shoulder, stands up and begins to pace with her, up and back, up and back, cooing and jiggling as she walks.

Watching, I think, I was not like that as a girl. I'd been as indifferent to babies as I'd been to dolls.

So why am I so relieved not to have miscarried?

It would have solved all my problems.

I slip into yet another mulling-over of the ingredients of my life and drift so far that the shout from the hall gives me a start. The girl and infant veer out of pattern towards the door, which opens. In comes the smell of toast followed by the sight of Siobhan bearing a tray. The boy trails her, carrying my handbag over his shoulder, dragging it along as if it weighs half a ton. Behind him shuffles in the dog with the rheumy eyes.

On the tray, which is set on my lap, is an awful lot of food: tea, a glass of milk, toast, an egg and a large bowl of porridge. While I am working out where to begin Siobhan points at the porridge: 'That's the important bit,' she informs me. Then, leaving Marie Louise to pace with the baby and the boy to torment the dog, she sits down on the foot of the bed, locates a pack of Marlboro and box of matches hidden under the toast plate, and lights up. On the first inhale she relaxes back so that her head is resting against the wall.

On the exhale she says, 'This your first one?'

I feel heat rising from the base of my neck. My throat fills. I nod.

She smiles. 'What do you want, a boy or a girl?'

I manage to nod again.

She waves her arm back and forth through her smoke. 'That's how I felt. "Give me anything," I used to say, "as long as it's alive." I miscarried the first time – *awful* it was. I nearly miscarried Shona too. Staying in bed the third month – that made the difference. That and prison porridge.'

She can't possibly know I haven't been exactly thrilled about my condition, and I know she can't know, but her certain assumption that I must be delighted makes me guilty about the truth. It's as if, having used the wart-sized bunch of cells inside me as an excuse to save my self, I ought to return the favour.

'I'm grateful to you for not abandoning me,' I say, reaching for the spoon and dipping it into the porridge. It's glutinous stuff – you can imagine it holding your insides together.

For a few minutes I eat and she smokes and stares into the smoke. Then the baby begins to wail again in a new note and, stubbing out the butt of her cigarette, Siobhan lifts her sweater, undoes her bra, reaches for the crying baby and plugs its mouth on to her right nipple.

I put aside the spoon and drink from the mug of tea.

– Heaven –

I am revived.

She says, 'Your friend – is she called Theresa? We got word to her. She's going to stay on in Belfast until you're OK to travel.'

'Who determines *that*?'

'The midwife. She'll be by later this morning.'

My sense of relief is complete. *A midwife – someone who knows.*

She says, 'You fell at this strange angle' and, within the limits of breast-feeding, raises her arms into a chaotic position. 'You skidded on the gravel too. Do your hands hurt?'

I extend my fingers and inspect the ripped nails. They do look painful, it's true, but I shake my head. 'Look,' I say, giving my throat a good clear, 'about those questions I started to ask you before I was so inconveniently indisposed...'

'They can wait,' she cuts in. 'You should be concentrating on one thing and one thing only at the moment... Listen, be a love would you and pass me that other cup of tea?'

I retrieve it from the tray and hand it to her. 'Yes, well, maybe I should be, but I can't.'

She tilts her head back to drink, then afterwards shrugs. 'Suit yourself.'

I decide to do that. I say, 'I'm here representing a woman who's been accused of killing another woman. Both of them were involved in the women's peace camp outside the American nuclear missile base at Moleham Heath.'

'I have a question,' she interjects; she is wriggling back into the comfortable spot at the end of the bed, which she now locates. 'What is a Yank doing working for English solicitors?'

'I don't work "for" them; I work "with" them.' I sound defensive, I can hear myself. 'I've been in London a long time,' I add for good measure.

'*Why* for God's sake?'

Her tone – half sarcastic, half incredulous – nearly goads me to an even stiffer come-back; my mouth is actually opening to let it out. Then, suddenly, I see flicker past an image of myself as she must see me: I dwell among the oppressor Brits not because I was born one and can't help myself; I am among them voluntarily.

My bristles relax.

I say, 'Believe it or not it seemed to me a more enlightened country – it *was* a more enlightened country at the time I arrived. The Vietnam War was still going on and to someone of my age and temperament there was nothing more shameful.' I stare at my broken nails, which seem to dissolve into a mist of memories. How had it all become so long ago? 'In fact, looking back I didn't so much come to England as leave America.'

Her reply is instant. 'But you got into it.' Her effort to sound neutral is as marked as the accusation it doesn't quite hide and it makes me wonder: can disillusionment with nationalism be explained to someone who feels robbed of their nation? If so, this can't, it seems to me, be the moment to try.

'I settled if that's what you mean,' I say. 'No matter how "in" it I appear, though, I'll never be "of" it – it *can't* make me feel ashamed ... I think that must be why I stay.' I decide it's time to go back to the subject. 'Where's my bag?' I ask, looking down towards the floor and speaking to the boy. When he doesn't appear to hear me I put the question again a little louder, but it is only when Siobhan says 'Declan' in a firm sub-parental tone that he stops scratching the dog's belly long enough to pick the bag off the floor and heave it to me.

It opens when it lands on the bed and as I stuff wallet and cheque book and brush and the rest of my bits back into it I see that the photo too is still there. I lift the tray away and set it on the bedside table, then put the bag on my lap in its place, my hands clasped on top of it. It fills the role of talisman, helping me rise above the sense of helplessness that comes with being bedridden like this, returning to me a semblance of my professional confidence.

I clear my throat yet again. 'The two women, the victim and the accused, were friends – you could even say they were good friends – but what the police want to say, *are* saying, is that on top of this they were lovers and that the death was the result of a lovers' quarrel. Now my client *is* a lesbian but the case against her is purely circumstantial – fuelled, I suspect, by a lot of anti-gay prejudice.'

She mutters something which I can't make out, though it sounds a bit snide.

'I'm sorry?' I say.

She waves her hand, unwilling to repeat the remark.

I can hardly force her so I let it pass. 'The point is, the dead woman wasn't a lesbian anyway.'

She grunts. 'Just one of those peace camp people.'

Again hearing scorn, I give her a look that says I want an explanation.

This time she's less reticent. Oblivious of the feeding baby, she leans towards me. 'This community has had its share of delegations visiting from peace camps and they have always – *always* – been shown the same hospitality as every other group:

they've been billeted and fed in peoples' homes and asked only for costs, they've been taken out to ceilidhs, they've been given the complete guided tour of the front line. And what thanks do they give? They call us *murderers* . . . No – really – I swear it to you. Ask my friend Briege if you don't believe me. She tried to get one of them to stop chanting an anti-military song when the Brits stopped their coach for an inspection and the bloody woman stood up and told her she wasn't about to "take orders from a killer".'

Siobhan looks sickened as she recites the line and I make the mistake of trying to conciliate. 'But the reputation of the IRA for violence –'

She rolls her eyes. 'Mother of Mary, two of Briege Reilly's brothers have been shot dead by the RUC, one was wounded by the army, her grandmother was crippled by a Loyalist attack on her local post office, her father has been shot three times – by the RUC, the Prods and the Brits – why does *she* get called the criminal?'

She leans even further towards me. 'And then these bloody so-called pacifists have the cheek to tell us that the first priority of the women's movement is abortion on demand.'

The baby gets the point even more forcefully than I do and is clearly fed up being squashed. Not only that, she's wet.

The girl Marie Louise has vanished so Siobhan turns to me. The nappies are downstairs – would I? I hold out my arms, which enfold this smelly parcel. The baby instantly stops crying and, head wobbling, stares into my face. One hand begins to bat me around the nose. As we gurgle at each other I find myself wondering despite myself what a mixture of David and me would look like. One shoe off and one shoe on? Probably.

Siobhan returns before I've appreciated she's been away and it's only when she's taken her child back and I'm physically on my own again that I recollect her animosity towards peace camp women. Now that I come to think about it I don't know why I'm surprised: the anarchic faction of the movement has always put off lots of other women in England too. Here they've obviously left the dominant impression, in which case Siobhan's view must be shared by a considerable portion of the republican activist community. And if this is right, if her view *is* widespread, then the

135

IRA would presumably have had few qualms about planting one of their members in a peace camp.

. . . And even fewer about planting a person called Annie Murphy.

I watch Siobhan stand up and, with Shona nestled against one shoulder, begin to pace again, up and back then up once more. Does she know I've figured it all out? Is she just challenging me in order to wind me up?

Is it not maybe time for the confrontation?

She seems to be feeling the same impatience when she suddenly says to me over the top of the baby's head, 'You think I'm involved with this.'

'After a manner of speaking,' I reply. I open the handbag and withdraw the print, which I am careful to keep covered with my palm. 'The victim disappeared the same morning your father's arrest was reported – just after she'd had a look at the paper.'

She's half the room away but I see her roll her eyes. '*That* is evidence?'

'No, but it was enough to suggest a connection that couldn't be dismissed out of hand, no matter how outrageous it seemed. I had to investigate it and when I did I found out that the dead woman's foster parents were Irish, that she'd wandered around on her own, with a camera, inside the American missile base on numerous occasions, and – most telling of all – that the security services put a D-notice on the press reporting of the story.'

Siobhan ceases her pacing when she reaches my bedside and stares down at me, eyes wide, jaw dropped. I find it hard for a moment to decide whether she's seriously impressed or putting me on and her tone doesn't enlighten me. 'You're not thinking . . .' she begins, 'I don't believe you're thinking . . .' Then her mouth lifts into a great broad grin of amusement, dispelling the ambiguity.

I refuse to be swayed by her mockery, which I recognise as an evasion tactic. What the hell, in her position I'd use an evasion tactic myself. I continue, 'I went to the Records Office here this afternoon – yesterday afternoon? whenever it was – to see if I could find any kind of link between the dead woman's foster parents, who were called Christine and Joseph Murphy and lived in Glasgow, and your father.'

Her grin seems to stiffen ever so slightly. '*Did* you now.'

'Yes,' I nod. 'I didn't find one . . .'

'Ah.'

'. . . but I got into the death records . . .'

'Oh?'

'. . . and I discovered something else just as useful.' I point to the area around her nose, then turn over the old photo of Annie and her mother and point to the same area in the face of the girl.

Almost imperceptibly Siobhan's coolness wavers and she glances away.

'I have to admit to you,' I go on, 'that it hadn't occurred to me to question the story about your mother and your younger sister being killed by a firebomb. After all, a reputable journalist got it straight from your father. The fact that the torso of the woman who died as Annie Murphy had been covered in scarring from fifteen- or sixteen-year-old burns – this existed as a separate piece of information . . . Until I checked and found no paperwork to support either of their deaths.'

She nods as if to say, do tell – how interesting – and lifts her gaze again. She stares into my eyes, studying me, defying me to break the contact. 'And this has led you to – what?'

I hold on. 'To turn their deaths around and see them as a good cover story; to realise that your father, your sister and possibly your mother as well were as involved with the IRA in Scotland and England as you and your brothers were here – as involved as your grandfather and uncles and cousins all were; and to understand that for reasons best known to your people, they gave your sister the job of infiltrating a peace camp, living among women whose values none of you had any particular respect for . . .'

Siobhan is beginning to laugh, which once more I put down to tactics and ignore. '. . . where she was uncovered not by the other women but by the CIA.'

The laugh grows. Is that hysteria I hear creeping in? It's something odd, and I hasten to finish. 'They must have killed her in the course of questioning her – hit her too hard, *some*thing –

then staged an accident to cover it up. My client had the ill fortune to walk into their scenario at the wrong moment.'

She's laughing so hard she has to put the baby back on the bed to avoid shaking it awake again.

All at once I recognise the undertone and react to it before I can stop myself: damn it, even if I *am* at a disadvantage, I won't be patronised. 'Oh for heaven's sake,' I complain.

She tries to contain herself and starts to succeed.

'You can't deny she was your sister, surely,' I say shortly.

Her laughter comes to a halt. 'Why not? She denied I was hers.'

My peevishness goes. 'Excuse me?'

'What I mean,' she says, 'is you had the beginning of it right, but after that . . .' She makes a snake of her hand and veers it off course. 'They both *did* survive the firebomb, though in my mother's case everyone's been wondering why ever since. She was only twenty-nine when it happened, you know? Young, active – what you'd expect.' She snaps her fingers. 'The next instant she was this drooling old woman with a mental age of eight who couldn't look after herself, never mind any of us.'

'Where is she?'

'In Dublin – with one of our cousins who's a nurse. My sister, her injuries were all on the surface. She needed special burns treatment, grafts and such like, and my father got given the money to fly her over to this special hospital in Glasgow.'

' "Got given" it by whom?'

Instead of answering she arches her right brow at me and stares into my eyes as if to say, 'You really need to ask?'

I realise I don't. 'He had no trouble entering Scotland?'

She shakes her head. 'There was no such thing as an exclusion order back in 1970. And anyway, he'd already convinced the security services that his response to being a sectarian target was to get out of Ireland. It's what a lot of people do, and he'd gone on record rubbishing the IRA' – she pronounced it 'Rah' – 'so they were satisfied. That's what made him so useful. He was the movement's first "sleeper" on the mainland. He stayed in Scotland while my sister was having her operations – she needed about six – then left her in the care of the cousins who gave her their name and enrolled her in convent school. He went down to

Liverpool where he changed his identity – even did some voice lessons to lose his accent – and stayed out of Irish circles. It was about ten years, I think, before he began operating for us actively.'

'I am amazed he was still willing. Ten years is a long time – especially if you're safe somewhere else and doing well.'

She shrugs. 'In actual fact the longer he lived in England the more political he got.'

'But his argument was with the Protestants in Northern Ireland surely. It wasn't the English who firebombed your family.'

'No, not literally, but the North is a British colony. Divide and rule is a strategy the British have used all over the world. Look at India and Pakistan; look at Israel and Palestine. The only way to change the status quo is to get the British voter to demand it.'

'And what would you want if that happened?'

'A united Ireland. Independence. The civil liberties you take for granted.'

'And you think violence is the best way to get them?'

' "Best"? I don't know "best", but as the state is using violence against us, it's the only way.'

I don't attempt to argue this because I can't. I return to the subject. 'Did you see your father after he left?'

She nods.

'Did she see him?'

She nods again.

'So she knew – ah – what he was involved in?'

'He pretended that she didn't until last year. He liked to think she could be kept out of it all – live what he called a normal life. He thought she deserved that because of what she'd already suffered. He believed that she believed he'd changed his identity to avoid the troubles – to avoid being Irish and being hassled by the police whenever they needed to round up a load of Paddies.' She sighs and I hear regret. 'If he'd told her the truth in the beginning he might have talked some sense into her when she decided male violence was the root of all evil.' She shakes her head. 'I couldn't believe it the time I saw her three years ago. We hadn't met up since we were kids, we had two days together, and what does she do? She spends the whole of the second day trying to persuade me of the errors of my ways – as if I had a lot of bloody choice.'

I open my mouth to speak but find my tongue has gone dry on me. How had I convinced myself that Annie Murphy was *either* a genuine peace woman *or* a relative of Gerard Ryan? Why had it never crossed my mind that she might be both?

Answer: because as an hypothesis it pointed me to no culprit, that's why.

I feel a sudden bewilderment. Can it be that this whole tack has been a complete and utter waste of time?

I can't let myself believe it. 'God,' I mumble, working up saliva in the half prayer, 'God.' I frown at her. 'Her death – if it's not connected to your father . . .'

'Did I say that?' she cuts in as she reaches to the tray for her cigarettes. She pulls one out and taps it on the box, first one end, then the other, watching her fingers absently.

I wait.

At last she puts it to her mouth and strikes a match to it. Her jaw looks tense to me. "I don't know for a fact what's connected to what. I've heard no official word at all.' She bites into the smoke. 'Only rumour.'

I give her an encouraging look but she just puffs quietly for a while, her eyes directed on her sleeping baby. Then, abruptly snapping to, she reaches under the bedside table and pulls out a stool which she straddles. 'The thing you need to understand,' she tells me, 'is that my father's felt guilty about my sister's injuries ever since they happened. It's based on nothing – he knows some mad Protestant Loyalist let off the bomb – but he feels it and because he feels it he's never, ever, been able to see her for who she is. He could have huge rows with her about politics, he could listen to her go on and on about pacifism, it didn't matter – when it came down to it she was family and he trusted her. That's why when he caught pneumonia last winter he asked her to come to Liverpool and look after him. And she went.' She flicks a column of ash into one of our empty cups: merely thinking about this wearies her. 'She was there for the next three months. She was around when his fever was so high he was delirious; she met most of his contacts, including three of the members of his cell; she knew where he kept his papers.'

She stubs her cigarette out in a hiss of cold tea and stands up again. Scratching under the sleeve of her jumper at her left forearm, she says, 'After his arrest was announced she visited him at Brixton. They were heard arguing. She was heard weeping. She was the only relative they let him see.' Then she turns around and walks over to the window and peers around the edge of the curtain, out into the morning.

I close my eyes and wait while the pieces rearrange themselves in my mind, this one going from a to b, that one going from e to f. When they stop I have a picture which is the exact inverse of the old.

Not only was Annie Murphy not an IRA plant inside the peace movement, there to organise some international act of terror, she was actually a peace movement spy inside the IRA.

Which means – *what?*

Which means at the very least that she used emotional blackmail on her father to persuade him to talk, or, at the very most – at the very most, talked herself.

Talked.

Talked as in 'snitched', 'grassed', 'revealed secret security information to the (British) authorities', 'spilled the beans'.

'Informed' or aided and abetted the action thereof.

I counsel myself to slow down, not to race ahead, but I can't help it now. A piece of common knowledge – of popular mythology – beckons: in the IRA's value system (it goes) informing is the worst of all crimes.

And Annie Murphy was not only guilty of it, she for some reason was walking around unprotected.

Seven

The midwife told me how lucky I was and forbade me to think about anything that might induce stress for the next twenty-four hours. Instantly I thought, how ironic – imagine saying *that* under the circumstances – and almost as quickly realised how much stress is induced by an appreciation for irony.

'If only I could,' I sighed.

'You must pretend you're on holiday,' she said as she departed, and before I could think about *that* too much there was a knock on the door and a man in the same thick lenses as Marie Louise and her brother Declan entered bearing the television set from downstairs. His name was also Declan and this was his house. His wife Geraldine and her sister, whose name I never caught, came up to check on me and left a single early daffodil, and a man named Martin who turned out to be the uncle I'd displaced from his room pulled up a chair and proceeded to lay out for me a potted history of the colonial relationship between the British and the Irish over the past four hundred years. Siobhan came and went, leaving the baby with me whenever she could get away with it; the dog adopted the spot in front of my door; Marie Louise practised her flute; and Martin returned with a photocopy of an impossible-to-get book about British military strategy in Ireland and a volume of poems about imperialism. No sooner would I finish food than there would be tea and no sooner would I finish tea than there would be food. In between I napped, getting up only to walk the six steps down to the next landing to use the toilet and the sink.

Eventually, after what seemed simply another quick snooze in an unending cycle of eat, drink, talk, play with the baby, nap, I resurfaced to find my clothes, now washed and ironed, in a neat pile on the bedside table. An hour later, after a last lingering tea, and with an unexpected pang of reluctance, I put on my coat, slipped my handbag strap over my shoulder and walked along the hall towards the front door. There I turned, gave the baby one more kiss and stooped to hug Marie Louise (who hugged back) and Declan (who ducked away). As I rose Siobhan put her free arm around my shoulders and squeezed. 'Well, Dee the Yank, good luck. Let me know what you have.'

After playing along with her assumptions for however long it had been – two days or more – this wasn't the moment to argue. 'Of course, sure – and thanks again. If you'd left me there . . .'

She laughed and gave me a quick kiss on each cheek. 'If I ever get arrested in England, can I ring you?'

I said I hoped she'd ring me if she ever managed to get into England, full stop; then I let Martin take my arm and lead me outside into the morning towards a banged-up old Cortina parked at the kerb.

It was the act of being handed over to strange men, followed by their brusque instruction to get in the back and keep my head down, that reminded me where I'd been all this time. I needed to be taken to Theresa – she had not been allowed to know where I was – and they were making damn certain I'd never be able to direct myself, her or anyone else back to wherever I'd been.

Yet in spite of this subterfuge and the nervousness it aroused, the journey was straightforward: they drove me almost to the airport, pulled in near a bus stop, and when a black cab emerged in the distance, saw that I caught it. The idea was that Theresa would meet me at the British Airways counter and sure enough, when I arrived, there she was in the distance, anxiously looking around.

I hurried towards her and as we held each other I felt a great weight lift from my shoulders – *almost over, almost home* – but alas I had barely reassured her that I was fine, and was on the point of answering the first of her questions (Did I feel OK about the pregnancy? Did David know?) when a small man with thin, slicked-down hair in a dark crumpled suit emerged beside us. If he'd been a contestant on *What's My Line?* I'd have guessed accountant, not because I know any who look like that but because that's how they're supposed to look. The ID with his picture on it clipped to his lapel said his name was John Jones; what he wanted was that we should follow him please, there were one or two security questions.

Theresa bit her lip at me and I had time to bite mine back before he gestured us through what appeared to be a cupboard door, down a corridor and through another door. Here we were separated and as I was led into a small interrogation cubicle containing the customary table and two chairs, I worked at composing myself. I couldn't name names because of my hopeless memory – this was the line I'd agreed to before the trip, and given that no illegal acts had been committed in my presence by any of my hosts, I would stick to it without guilt.

Where had I stayed? West Belfast somewhere. Who with? Mary and John Something. Who'd picked me up at the airport? A taxi. Who'd shown me around? My colleague in the other interrogation room. Who had I met? Sorry, I was hopeless with names. Where had I stayed? As I'd said earlier, west Belfast. And so it went on, the same questions repeated first in the same order, then backwards, then from the middle. John Jones didn't seem to know about my fainting spell in the car park of the Republican club or my contact with Siobhan Ryan, or if he did he wasn't letting on. Was I really going to get out of this so lightly?

He said, 'Now – the purpose of your visit.'

'I'm investigating a defence case,' I replied. I thought that sounded vague enough – unspecific but true.

Nodding, he flipped a couple of pages in his pad, skimmed and said, 'A lesbian murder.'

Do not be provoked, I told myself. Do not show surprise. It's his business to know my business. 'My client's sexuality is irrelevant,' I said. 'She's been charged with a murder she didn't commit.'

The obvious next question was, 'How does this connect to Belfast?' and I geared myself for it. Instead he said, 'What's your evidence?'

I bristled. 'That's privileged. You know that.'

He smiled and described to me the approximate contents of my pathologist's report.

I was more bewildered than appalled. Why was he teasing me this way? He had to know about the link between Annie Murphy and Gerard Ryan – these people knew everything. And if he didn't know, why wasn't he quizzing me about the Maire Kelly case?

He said, 'Can the dirt on the dead woman's clothing be traced to a particular place?'

I thought, what the hell, and admitted I had no idea but hoped so, obviously.

He went back to his initial question and took me through the sequence again once – twice – a third time, varying the order, prying a little more here and a little more there, not seeming to mind that I never told him more than he knew when we started out. In this way we passed a half hour – an hour – an hour and a half – on the subject of Gillian Shiraz and the forensic evidence of her innocence. Increasingly I got the feeling that he'd simply had a boring day and was shootin' the breeze to fill a block on his time sheet. Finally he seemed to decide he'd used up enough, shook my hand, told me how fascinating he'd found our meeting, and escorted me to the check-in desk in time for the mid-day flight to Heathrow.

Theresa boarded just before take-off, her face gaunt with suppressed anger. *She* had spent two hours fielding questions about Gerard Ryan and about the alleged IRA members she'd be defending against his alleged allegations.

We stopped in at University College Hospital on the way back from the airport at Theresa's insistence, and though I opened my mouth to argue, I closed it without saying anything. It wasn't, however, until I was lying half naked on my back on the examining table, feet in the stirrups, knees spread, trying as always not to let the inherent humiliation of the proceedings get to me, that I admitted to myself that somehow at some point over the past couple of days I had made a decision: not only was I relieved not to have miscarried, I wanted to have this baby.

It was a mad thing – a totally irrational certainty so beyond the range of my capacity for argument that I was quite awed at myself for containing such a force. I'd thought all that animal residue had been civilised out of me years ago. And who would have expected that when the doctor told me I should give myself another week on my back in bed and take it slow for at least another week after that, I would begin instantly planning how I was going to reorganise my work?

– My work which suddenly and for the first time in years did not seem the centre of my universe.

What had Siobhan Ryan and her household done to me?

Claudine was waiting with Theresa when I came out. 'Suze sent me,' she said, miming a pull on an invisible forelock. 'At your service.'

When we were all in her car and she'd manoeuvred it out into the traffic, she glanced over at me with all of her youth in her eyes. 'We were incredibly worried about you,' she said. 'When we heard that you'd collapsed and were being held in a *safe house* by an *Irish terrorist* – the daughter of this *supergrass*. . .'

I thought: but it wasn't like that at all; those are the phrases we use here but they are the wrong phrases; they evoke the wrong pictures.

I cut in with a heat I hadn't expected. 'I was very well looked after actually. Siobhan Ryan went out of her way to make sure I was OK.'

Obviously stung, she squeezed out an 'Oh' (or maybe it was an 'Oh?'), then started talking about something completely different.

I hadn't meant to bite at her – where had it come from? But I couldn't summon the energy to stop, go back, get into it. It was too soon. I didn't know what to say; didn't have the vocabulary to say it.

Not yet.

We spent the rest of the bumper to bumper journey from Warren Street to Marylebone discussing the depth of the files and the pile of phone messages waiting on my desk, and going through the most urgent of the problems. My mind felt nimble the way it does after I've been on a holiday: solutions arose easily and the problems had no power to sink hooks into me. When I put them down they stayed down.

My own problems, too, seemed less excruciatingly burdensome for having been set aside and by the time Suze came by that evening I felt I had answers where before there'd been fog.

She arrived bearing a bag of groceries and some cut flowers and for the first ten minutes or so she rushed around finding a vase and making tea and cooking me the toast and poached egg she insisted I needed. Finally she filled a mug for herself, sat down at the end of the bed, kicked off her shoes and leaned back. She was taking her first sip when her eye fell on the copy of *Natural Childbirth* that I'd set to one side on the bed cover. She swallowed the wrong way and began to cough.

I rescued her mug and hit her on the back a couple of times. She wasn't even fully recovered when she said, 'So you've decided – decided to go through with it?'

I laughed. 'I wish you wouldn't make it sound like suicide, Suze. I'm just going to have a baby.' It was the first time I'd said it out loud and I discovered I quite liked the ring of it: it sounded right; it even sounded like me.

'Sorry,' she said. 'I must have been projecting.' She took back her tea. 'Does David know yet?'

I shook my head. 'He's passing through at the weekend – I'll tell him then. I reckon I'll be on my own with it.'

Suze widened her eyes at me, like she couldn't quite believe it was me saying this, then glanced away and began to pluck at the threads of the bed cover, thinking. I could imagine what was going through her mind: how would the firm manage next year with both Simone *and* me away on maternity leave? Would we be able to find temp help? Was she going to have to give up her police committee work? She didn't say any of this, however. Instead she straightened and, giving me a funny kind of stiff smile, cleared her throat. 'Can I be aunty?'

I laughed and held out my arms to her. 'Listen, you can be mommy.'

As she leaned down to accept the hug, she loosened and laughed as well. 'That's OK. Aunty will do.' Then she stuck out a hand to me and we shook on it. 'Now,' she said, 'tell me about Belfast.'

The words I hadn't been able to find earlier with Claudine now seemed to come effortlessly, fuelled by a sense of outrage I didn't know I'd acquired until I heard it in my voice. When I eventually began to wind down, Suze whistled as if to say well I'll be damned. 'Well I'll be damned,' she said, 'you've had *your* head turned around.'

'It was impossible not to. Being there, seeing how people are forced to live – I understood why the Catholics in the North were so inspired by the American black civil rights movement in the late sixties. The parallels are so clear – the racism in the North – but I've never really seen it that way before. The Anglo Saxon English ruling class has played divide and rule among two tribes, the Irish Celts – the natives – and the Scottish Celts, who they began to plant in Ulster in the early seventeenth century. If the working-class Loyalists would only just realise how they've been used . . .'

But Suze had started laughing, not at me exactly but about me and I had a sudden appreciation of how I must sound. The zeal of the convert: put me in Downing Street for a single day, make me Northern Ireland Minister, I'll sort it out. I slumped back against the pillow, smiling because she was right, it *was* pretty amusing, but I couldn't stop myself adding, 'OK, OK, but you have to admit, Suze, that if those people were black or Latin or Palestinian or Polish or even just further away, the whole of the liberal establishment would be competing with the left to organise benefit rock concerts.'

'You're probably right; unfortunately for them, though, they're Irish and just across a narrow bit of sea. They've also been fighting this war for too long.'

'That's hardly their fault.'

'Not their fault – their tragedy. They've been forced to fight then been corrupted by the violence – so corrupted they use it more and more indiscriminately.'

The image of Annie's neck rose in my mind: I wouldn't have called that indiscriminate. And as for the cover-up . . .

A chill blew up my spine.

How could I contain in myself *both* a respect for Siobhan and everyone else I'd met in Belfast *and* a moral horror at some of the steps they felt driven to?

Didn't they feel the same horror? Had anyone claimed to enjoy the violence?

A headache began to rear up out of my confusion and as much to fend it off as anything else I sighed and said, 'To think I went over there worried that Annie was killed because she was IRA and came away worried that she was killed because she wasn't. No, not "worried": *certain*.'

Suze nodded and seemed about to say something but stopped as if the words weren't there and instead just mumbled 'hmmm' and frowned at her fingers for several moments, watching them pick at a thread on the fraying edge of the chair arm. Eventually she jerked her attention back and her head up and said 'More tea?' and was on her feet and on her way into the kitchen even before my predictable response. When she returned with the fresh pot the frown hadn't lifted.

'They haven't claimed credit,' she said. 'The IRA usually claim credit.'

This hadn't occurred to me. 'Maybe they tried,' I countered. 'There *is* a D-notice on the story, don't forget.'

She blew into her cup, brows still pinched together across the bridge of her nose – 'Mmmm, maybe' – then tried to take a sip of the steaming liquid. It was still too hot. 'It's not the IRA's style though either. They shoot informers in the kneecaps and leave them in public places. The whole object of the exercise, the way I've always understood it, is to spread the word. Staging a phoney accident as a cover-up – it doesn't make sense.'

Here was something *else* I hadn't wondered about. And I felt a sudden strong resistance to doing so, even a resentment at being asked. Damn Suze and her need to try to unpick the tightest of one's pet theories. I didn't want the bold light of her reason; I was happy with the shutter closed.

I said, 'It goes with the D-notice.'

The frown turned sharp. 'You think the *police* are covering it up?'

Did I? It was certainly the implication of what I'd said. I shrugged. 'The Home Office obviously wants to keep the lid on this particular internal IRA vendetta.'

'Why?'

I shrugged again. 'Who knows? Presumably it has to do with their testimony deal with Gerard Ryan.'

'But it was Annie Murphy who grassed, not Gerard Ryan – that's what you just told me. They've got themselves somebody who isn't going to testify in court when it comes to it.'

My impatience with her was rising quite unaccountably. I didn't want to have to think about these things; why was she making me think about these things? 'Yes, well, that's their problem,' I grumbled. 'What's bothering me is mine. What the hell am I going to *do* with what I know?'

'What can you do? You haven't any proof.'

'I could try to collect it.'

'Against the IRA? Are you out of your mind?'

'But if they're guilty of murder . . .'

'War crimes – they're fighting back and these are war crimes. They've merely killed a traitor who betrayed them to the authorities. That's what you implied not two minutes ago.'

'But "merely killed" is still killed – as *you* implied not two minutes ago.' My mind was now so overstretched by this tugging both ways that it made my head feel heavy. My chin dropped against my chest. I closed my eyes. How could I possibly deal with this? I was too fragile for Big Issues, especially this damned if you do, damned if you don't variety.

Tears rose suddenly like they can, and one got out and began to slide down my cheek. Angrily I swiped at it.

Suze leaned forward and caught my wrist. 'Dee – listen – don't,' she said softly. 'You don't need to get into this – I'm sorry I got you going.' She squeezed my hand, then let it go, reached for her bag and found a tissue for me. 'I should have told you straightaway – Mary Mackay rang. She's examined Annie's clothes at last – apparently the Home Office gave her a harder time about them than about the body. She's been made to deal with some official there she's never heard of before. Anyway, the nature and the pattern of the grit on the jacket and jeans suggest, she says, an outdoor fall, probably on to gravel, probably from a height of at least thirty feet. With a little more of that you'll be able to get Gillian off on the technicalities.'

'Come on Suze,' I sniffed, almost but not quite in control

again. 'You can't duck a moral dilemma just because you don't like it.'

'Maybe, but there's no need to walk out into the middle of the road and stand in its way – especially when you're under instructions to relax.'

'But . . .'

'No, no buts. It's not your job to find out who killed Annie, only to establish that Gillian didn't – just keep telling yourself that.'

I promised to try.

I

At 3.45 the following afternoon Gillian Shiraz rang me from the phone booth on the Holloway Road to thank me for getting her out. She was so excited she didn't want to know that I hadn't the first idea what she was talking about. She was off to see Katy, that was all that mattered – that and her new resolve. No longer did she fear the prospect of facing her ex-husband in court, or of arguing with him over custody.

'I'm looking forward to it,' she announced. Then her money ran out.

After my surprise had worn off and I'd confirmed the situation with the police, relaxation ought to have come easier to me, and of course to the extent that I was under much less pressure, it did. My client was out of danger – I could move on to other things free of the vision of an innocent woman rotting in jail. What couldn't be so lightly dropped with the charges, however, was the vision of Annie Murphy on the floor of her room with her neck at that impossible angle.

Two things niggled: the suspicion that I'd been got rid of and the memory of that odd security interview I'd been put through leaving Belfast.

My third day at home, when I felt completely all right again but had this damn deal to honour, I walked over to Marylebone Station to buy a newspaper and on my way out stopped and rang George from one of the public phones.

'What's become of that possibility that Tonio Shiraz freelanced for British intelligence?' I asked him. His answer was that it seemed to be true.

I waited for meaning, for a neat fit of this piece into all the other pieces, but nothing happened. I again reminded myself that it was none of my affair, then detoured to the library, selected a couple of novels, and for the rest of the day managed to staunch the mental chatter.

The following morning Theresa rang to see how I was getting on and to ask when I thought I might feel up to visiting Maire Kelly, who had at long last been transferred down from Manchester and was eager to hear about my visit with her Belfast relatives. An hour later I arrived at the prison.

Brixton's smell is different from Holloway's, the difference between male and female sweat; and ammonia, unable to kill it, combines with it in a way that brings a lump of bile to the back of the throat. It made me walk more briskly than I had in several days.

I'd never been to the terrorist wing before and pushing through the double doors that led to it I thought, Annie Murphy walked through these same doors and along this same corridor to visit her father. An instant later a second thought made my feet come to a halt: I had taken Siobhan Ryan's word for this story because she'd gone out of her way to help me and I'd liked her. I had consciously ignored the fact that she was a convicted member of the IRA. Had I been right to trust her? Why *should* she have been straight with me?

When I reached the reception desk the uniformed guard wasn't at his post but standing some yards away talking to a workman in a boiler suit. At my arrival he merely glanced over his shoulder, said 'Sign the register please' and returned to his conversation.

I recognised the opportunity as I approached the open book. Skimming the two exposed pages I saw that the dates were too recent – if Annie had come the entry would be back a few – and ever so coolly I reached out and turned carefully, my eye moving quickly down the admissions column, name by name, page by page until, about two thirds of the way up the fourth page it was arrested by an entry printed clearly and in bold, black felt tip: 'A. Murphy' (it read), to visit 'G. Ryan'. The date was right – the day she'd disappeared after leaving Gillian's daughter Katy at the doctor – and her signature was there twice, once where she'd signed in and once where she'd signed out.

Siobhan *had* told me the truth. Any embryonic wild speculations about ulterior motives will please lie down.

I turned back to the current page, picked up the pen, filled in my own details and signed my name on the 'in' space. Then I stood there, tapping my fingernails on the desk, waiting for the guard to get around to me.

It wasn't my nails, though, but the sound of leather heels clicking on the floor tiles, getting louder and louder as their wearer approached, that broke up the conversation: the guard, the workman and I all turned around to see a man in a suit coming towards us, silk threads shining under the fluorescent strip lighting, briefcase under his arm. The workman saluted the guard with a wave and wandered away. The guard straightened and looked through me at the newcomer.

I am invisible, it occurred to me. That's why I got away with it. He can't really see me.

Either that or visitors are meant to make their way unescorted from here to the cells.

Unlikely as this seemed to me I stepped forward, just to provoke a response.

'Excuse me, Madam,' came a voice that could only have been acquired at an English boarding school.

I stopped and looked around at the man in the suit. 'Yes?'

He tapped the visitors' register. 'I believe you'll find it's customary to sign out as well as in.'

I frowned and turned to the guard. What a bizarre thing.

But he nodded and pointed to the corridor. 'It's one way,' he told me. 'You'll be seen out at the other end – you won't come back this direction.'

Still I resisted: I picked up the pen but couldn't do anything with it.

The guard looked amused; he was thinking *'women'* – you could see it in his eyes. 'It's not as if people are trying to break in here you know,' he laughed.

I sighed. Patronising manner or no, this was clearly true. I signed again in the 'out' column and waited while he called another guard to escort me to the interview room.

I'd built up a picture of Maire Kelly from talking to her relatives which turned out to be accurate. She was a calm young woman with a still centre so far unbent by the regular ritual of strip searching. She had faith in the firm, she said, as if it were a blessing; she would co-operate in any way she could. I promised to visit again, wished her well and made my way back out to the corridor. Two guards seemed to materialise out of the tiles, one at my right side, one at my left, and showed me through the back end of the wing to the outside.

The door had closed behind me and I was adjusting my scarf against the wind, letting my thoughts move around my mind as they would, when suddenly two of them were drawn to each other. The connection was perfect, so perfect a shock of realisation went through me.

I walked as fast as I could down to the High Street, found a phone that was working and rang Vic Phillips.

'Are you serious?' he said. The cigarette that had been en route to his mouth became a baton punctuating his indignation. 'You got me over here to tell me Theresa believes I'm being used by MI5?'

We were in Regent's Park again, this time standing by the edge of the fountain. It was a mild day, the first in weeks, and the frozen spouts of water that were supposed to gush in arches from the conch of the marble merman and the mouths of the fish in his honour guard had thawed into dribbles. The atmosphere felt heavy with germs on the point of waking up.

'She's an ally of yours,' I said. 'It's a significant defection.'
'Based on?'
'Logic. Gerard Ryan wouldn't grass, therefore anyone who says he has must have an ulterior motive.'
'And what are you saying? You're going with this?'
'I'm saying you put questions to your man inside for me. I need to be reassured about his answers.'

He pushed the cigarette into his mouth and in a single movement lit it with the lighter he'd been concealing in his palm. 'You weren't led astray were you?' he said on the exhale.

I shook my head: this was true. I cleared my throat and said a bit uneasily, 'The thing is, there's something else I want to test on him, something much . . .' – I searched for the word – '*bigger*. If there's even the remotest possibility he isn't who you think he is . . .'

'Dee, he and I go back five years. If he was going to drop me in it he could have done it on at least six occasions.' He leaned towards me and lowered his voice. 'Besides which, he's helping me with a story which believe me can have no other purpose than to make public a fact which will deeply embarrass this government.'

'Is this the one about the security services "disappearing" people down some bottomless pit in the countryside?' I whispered back.

It was obvious that he'd completely forgotten mentioning this to me and to hide his dismay he looked around again, now with self-mocking furtiveness. 'Did I say that? Who said that?'

I wiggled my finger in my ear. 'It must be me. I must be hearing things.'

'Which you can no longer recall.'

I put hand on heart. 'Which I can no longer recall . . . Vic, listen. I want to meet your guy. I *need* to meet him.'

He imitated my ear gesture.

'Really,' I said.

'Impossible,' he said, a spontaneous scowl getting the better of his charm. 'I'm surprised at you even asking. I'm happy to put whatever-it-is to him for you like I did before – isn't that good enough?'

'It's not a question of "good". It simply wouldn't be in your interests for me to use you as a go-between on this. It wouldn't be fair to let you in on something you'll never be able to publish.'

' "Never"? Surely not "never". Don't you know me better than that Dee? I'm quite used to waiting.'

I stared in at the muzzy orange forms moving indolently beneath the thinning ice of the shallow pool. Deep down I had expected him to say this. I'd have been amazed, really, if he hadn't.

'OK,' I said, looking over at him again. 'But don't say I didn't warn you.' I took a large breath of the heavy air. 'I think it's possible Annie Murphy was abducted from inside Brixton Prison when she visited her father; I think Special Branch or the anti-terrorist division could have taken her to question her and ended up killing her.'

Vic, cool old hack that he liked to come on, started to laugh, then realised I hadn't told a joke and stopped. His eyes bulged at me in a way that asked as much as it exclaimed and I read the question without any trouble.

'Visitors are made to sign in *and out* when they enter the terrorist wing at the prison. It would be easy enough to . . .'

But he saw it. He got to his feet, bent his arm, frowned at his wrist. 'Give me . . .' – he shook his watch – 'give me till tea time.' And squeezing me fraternally on the bicep, he threw his cigarette on the ground and strode away across the park.

Three hours later he rang me. 'I spoke to my friend about the matter we discussed. How does Trafalgar Square, tomorrow afternoon, four o'clock, sound?'

I said it sounded fine.

What I forgot when I decided to ignore the doctor's advice and go into the office the next morning was that everyone would want to have a chat and that chats can be tiring when your hormones are reorganising themselves; I also forgot that messages had been collecting for nearly a week and that picking up old pieces requires a lot of concentration. By lunchtime I could see myself running out of energy before the middle of the afternoon even arrived and, filling a bag with the most urgent of my files, retreated home.

I remember settling down on the sofa in the sitting room with a cup of tea by my side, legs stretched out, heels on coffee table, papers of a particularly prolonged immigration case on my lap; what I don't recollect is how much I read of the first paragraph before nodding off. When the flap of my letterbox banged and brought me back, it was twenty past three.

Through the peephole I saw a man of maybe forty-five or fifty in a blue boilersuit and flat cap carrying a bucket and ladder. He wasn't the usual window cleaner, but I opened the door. 'I'm sorry . . .' I started.

'I do free estimates, lady,' he said as his hand dipped into his bucket. 'You should let me in for a look.' He pulled out a piece of paper and held it up to me. 'Trafalgar Square impossible,' it said. He touched his index finger to his lips, then went on, 'Only £1.50 each.' He pointed into my sitting room. 'Bay window seats treated as one.'

I studied his face – the lines on the forehead, the shadows beneath the small close-set eyes, the deep grooves between the nostrils and the corners of the mouth. He was older than I'd for some reason imagined – older and stouter and less aristocratic. Closer to vagabond than James Bond, though that was partly the fault of his get-up.

I gestured him in and as I shut the door behind him he walked into the sitting room and went straight over to the fireplace. He felt around under the mantelpiece, found something, picked it off and held it up. It was a small black metal dot. Damn, I thought, how dare they invade my privacy. And what an idiot I was. I'd sensed my flat had been broken into when the case had started but had mistrusted my instinct and made a half-assed search.

He put the device back in place as he said, 'This room'll cost you a fiver and I'll do the bedroom for the same.' He held up a second note: 'Tell me, "Not now. I'm going out." '

'Not now, I'm going out.'

'OK, lady. I'm over here again next week. I'll call back. Here's my card.' He gave me a folded piece of paper which I thanked him for before I saw him out. This message said. 'A colleague is on to me. Give me five minutes, then leave and take the tube to Richmond. From there walk along the route I've marked on the attached map until you get to Dino's sandwich bar. I'll meet you there. Now please destroy this note.'

It made me feel ridiculous but after I'd read the message again and separated it from the photocopy of the page from the A-Z I took the bit of paper into the kitchen and set it alight over a burner on the gas stove. Then I went back out to the sitting room, picked up the phone and dialled Vic's office. He hadn't been in. When I tried his home number I got his answerphone.

I glanced at the clock: three minutes.

Why the nerves? You asked for this meeting.

I avoided further thought by counting the seconds to the end of the five minutes, and when I got there I put on my coat, scarf, hat and gloves and headed out. After locking my front door I slipped my ring of keys into my pocket, gave them a pat (my talisman) and made my way to Edgware Road station. I bought the evening paper and read it minutely on the way to Richmond.

Though west London is not my patch, Dino's was easy enough to find. I looked through the window and counted two people, an elderly woman eating from a soup bowl at a table by herself and, across the room in front of the cigarette machine, a teenage male. Neither was wearing a flat cap or dark boilersuit and I was wondering if this was the right place after all when a voice spoke at my ear. 'Thanks for coming.' I turned and looked into the face of the window cleaner, which this time looked back at me from beneath a toupé the texture and yellow colour of doll's hair. He was dressed in a mustard check sports jacket and jeans and seemed even stubbier and puffier in this guise. 'Let's go in, shall we?'

I pushed open the door and made for a small table in the corner. I started to slide into the padded bench facing the windows and entrance but he bent and asked me to let him sit there. I said sure and sat down in the chair instead.

'Coffee? Or would you prefer tea?' he said.

I said coffee and while he was getting it I turned in the chair and kept an eye out for Vic.

The man returned carrying two cups of coffee by their saucers. He set one in front of me, then set down his own and slid into the bench. 'My name's John by the way.' He stuck out his right hand.

I shook it and smiled. 'Hello John. We're expecting Vic I assume?'

'Actually we're not.' He tried his coffee, which was still too hot to drink, and put it back in the saucer. 'In fact he's probably still standing in Trafalgar Square.'

'Really? You picked me up but not him?'

'He's too risky. Now that my colleague's on to me it's impossible for me to meet Victor again . . . No – please – don't waste your sympathy. It was bound to happen sooner or later. I should have cut my losses and emigrated ages ago.'

'The consequences are that dramatic?'

'Are they? My God. Grassing on your mates is as heinous a

crime in the secret service as it is in the IRA.'

I somehow had no trouble believing this. 'Where will you go?'

'You don't want to know. The point is, I'll need two days to get it organised. My proviso for talking to you is that afterwards you must keep your lips sealed for at least those two days. Once I'm gone, if you want to get it confirmed and published or if you think you can use it to pursue a case in the courts, that's up to you.'

'Great, sure, I'll wait two days,' I said instantly. 'But speaking of risks – I mean, how can you be certain you can trust me?'

'Because I know *you*.' He smiled, then closed his eyes and swayed a bit like a medium. 'Name: Dee Street. Place of birth: Los Angeles. Father: a well-known lawyer, now sadly deceased. Mother: was his secretary, is now retired. Distinguishing physical feature: birthmark on right thigh. Marital status . . .'

'Enough,' I said.

'Health: suffers from allergies and vertigo. Status in UK: unrestricted visa. Length of residency . . .'

I put my hands over my ears. This really wasn't amusing. 'Please,' I said. 'I mean it.'

He stopped and turned up the smile to a grin. He had a yellow front tooth which matched his hair. 'Sorry,' he said. He leaned towards me. 'I want to show you the place where Annie Murphy was killed. You can take as many photos and dust samples as you like.'

'I don't have a camera.'

'I've got one in the car.' He picked up his cup and this time drank.

I picked up my cup as well but swivelled around with it so that I could look across the café and out the window again. It was very dark out there now. If there was a moon or stars their light was covered by cloud. I swivelled back so that I was facing him once more, and drank. I needed caffeine. 'How far is it from here?'

He scratched his head and the whole hair piece moved slightly from side to side. 'A ten-minute walk? Not very far.'

'I see,' I said. I reached for the bowl of sugar and spooned a heaping teaspoonful into my drink, then spent a moment stirring it. I never used sugar. 'I'm interested in what else you know about Annie Murphy's death.'

He glanced beyond my shoulder, scanned a moment and, apparently satisified, reached into the breast pocket of his jacket, from whence he withdrew a slender walkman. This he handed to me.

I peered in at the tape, which was labelled Vivaldi's 'Winter', and slipped the headset over my ears. Then I pushed the button, but instead of sweeping chords I heard a male voice with a Liverpool Irish accent saying: 'You mustn't ask that of me Anne Marie. You shouldn't have come here, it's what they wanted you to do, but now you're here you mustn't ask that.'

A woman's voice, higher and Scots-flavoured with an edge of distress in it said, 'I have to ask that. Look at yourself – you're ill, Da. I want you to live. Why do you protect them?'

'If I'm ill it's because I haven't slept for more than about half an hour at a stretch since they picked me up eight days ago. The Brits invented interrogation techniques – I've told you that. And as for why I keep silent, you know why. You wear the scars.'

'Yes, exactly, *I* wear them. They're *my* scars. If I want revenge for them I'll take it myself. They're your excuse for these years of violence, Da.'

His soft grunt was dismissive but he didn't otherwise rise to this. 'Listen Anne Marie, they will question you when you leave. You must keep the promise you made to me last year. You know nothing.'

'But that isn't true. I know . . .'

'Hush now, you're just a wee girl. The walls are listening.'

John leaned across and pressed the off button, then pulled the headset off me. He said nothing but his look was expectant.

I wasn't inclined to disappoint him. 'So *was* it Annie who talked, not Gerard?' I asked.

He shrugged. 'She knew very little our people didn't.'

'Then why did they abduct her?''

'Isn't it obvious? As a lever to crack him. The anti-terrorist division takes pride in its research. They – we – knew the lengths he'd gone to to protect her from the situation in the North, fostering her to cousins, insisting she go to a convent school out in the middle of nowhere in Scotland. Our intelligence on him was that he believed the scarring on her breasts and torso was going to make things difficult enough for her but was determined she should have an ordinary life: a husband, a baby, a house, a job. *Happiness*. The team in charge of his interrogation worked away at this angle and around about his fourth or fifth day in custody concluded that his feeling for her was definitely the route in to him.'

'But he has three other children.'

'Yes – none of whom was damaged by the firebomb.' He shrugged. 'I'm not a psychologist but I expect he saw her as the innocence he lost when, because of her injuries and his wife's, he took the fateful step and joined the Republicans . . . Anyway, what our people didn't know and couldn't extract from him was where she was – which is why they played up the importance of Ryan's arrest so much when they announced it to the media. The press thereafter did what we knew they'd do and ran it prominently, and she did what we hoped she'd do and showed up at the prison asking to see him the very morning the story broke.' He paused and tilted his head almost coyly at me. 'How did you figure that out, by the way?'

The figure of Siobhan came to mind and I thought, he may be a good guy but he's still MI5. I said, 'I'm clairvoyant – isn't *that* in my file?' Then I tried to push him back to what interested me. 'Are you going to tell me which of them informed?'

But he stayed in the frivolous mode. 'Ay,' he said, lifting his index finger in a Socratic gesture, 'there's the rub.'

I translated this to mean, Not yet, and tried another tack. 'How about, how did she die?'

'This is what I want to show you.' He knocked back the dregs and stood up, then fished in his pockets and put a couple of coins on the table.

I continued to sit. 'A ten-minute walk?'

'Along a well-lit street,' he said. When I carried on sitting he said, ' "Never trust a strange man"?'

'Something like that,' I agreed as I clasped my cup and swallowed the last drops of my coffee. I thought, I am fifteen years younger and fifteen pounds lighter than he is. Then I felt for

161

the keys in my coat pocket and pushed back my chair.

Heavy rain was falling and we had only my small black umbrella with the two broken spokes, so we concentrated on co-ordinating our feet and elbows and spoke only of immediacies. After eight or ten minutes of this agony, and just as my trainers were starting to take in water, he herded me left into a residential street of large late-Victorian semi-detached houses. Twenty yards later he stopped me by the open gate of a darkened four-storey specimen with a thicket of estate agency noticeboards out front. He looked in either direction and I did the same, but apart from a cat on the kerb opposite, saw no other street life. He started in the gate but before I could follow, paused, patted his pockets and scowled to himself. 'Hang on a tick.'

He went to a small black ex-post-office van parked about two doors down, unlocked the driver's door, fiddled about and came back. 'Keys,' he smiled, holding them up in one hand. 'Camera,' he said, holding it up in the other. Then he went on up the path and let us in.

The electricity had been turned off and there wasn't much natural light but he now produced a small flashlight from his pocket and the beam from that was good enough to help us see the stairs as we made our way up them. When we eventually reached the top an aeon later, we were faced with a selection of closed doors, but he immediately took hold of the knob of the middle one and pushed it open. Then he gestured me in.

I started to comply but paused first to look, only to be immobilised by what I saw. A single bed, a chair with clothes on it, a bedside table with a lamp and a couple of books – even the window seemed in the same relative position. For a moment I was in Belfast again but then he slid past me and brought me back.

I followed him to the window and when we got closer I realised the bottom pane of glass was missing. I looked out – got a quick sense of the long drop – and ducked back in. He was about an inch from me – too close – and I ducked away from him too.

'She fell from here,' he said. He stopped and pressed his fingers to the floor, then stood and displayed them to me. I could see the glint of the fine slivers.

I went over to the chair and sat down heavily. 'Why?'

'She was being watched by a baboon, that's why. She'd been interrogated solidly for forty-eight hours and had been given a sedative. All he had to do was stay at her side and watch her sleep. Instead he went to make a phone call. He ran back when he heard the glass shattering but she was over by that time. He saw her lose her grip and drop like a ragdoll. It's thirty feet down.'

The picture made my stomach heave; I sought relief in sarcasm. 'Had she been sufficiently milked?'

He feigned boyishness again. 'If I answer your question will you answer mine?'

This time when I thought of Siobhan I also thought, what the hell, apart from the occasionally mannered style, the guy seems to be levelling with me. It seemed a fair enough deal. 'Sure,' I nodded.

Unnervingly he leaned against the sill. 'I told you, what she knew wasn't the point. They were just using the fact that they had her to force him to do business with Her Majesty's government.'

'Names in return for her release?'

'Names and testimony at a series of trials in return for her release, and new identities for him and all of his family in Canada – not that anyone expected Siobhan or the brothers to go.'

'And did this blackmail work?'

'The official departmental line is yes. A birdy's told me they're still working on it.'

'How long would she have been held hostage?'

'Until the trial of the people charged on her father's evidence.'

'Which would have been announced as a supergrass trial regardless of whether or not he talked . . .'

'And is still scheduled to be so announced – you're catching on.'

'So why was Annie's body taken back and rearranged in her room?'

'That's two you'll owe me.'

I shrugged. I didn't have much to give away.

He said, 'It was done because the department wanted to be certain that, when Ryan finally did find out she was dead, it was clearly disassociated. The powers that be wanted proof on the record that they had let her go, that she'd been killed after she'd gone home. They wanted to make it absolutely impossible for people like your journalist friend Victor even to suggest the idea of death in custody. Staging the accident you discovered was no big deal.'

I thought of myself as pretty cynical but this was too much. 'But if it was staged as an accident, why frame someone?'

'Gillian Shiraz set herself up for the manslaughter thing by walking in at the wrong time.'

'You mean, when in doubt, blame the victim? They must have known about Gillian – she could have walked in when they were planting the body.'

'They had plans to distract her the way they distracted the neighbours with the Jehovah's Witnesses. What they didn't know about was that loud row she'd had on the telephone with her husband within earshot of that old boy downstairs.'

'Who just happens to be a member of the National Front?'

'Let's just say he's slightly overzealous.'

'And her husband – are you saying it was coincidence that he co-operated?'

'I'm saying they needed a bit of luck at that point. It was the head of operations' last operation. He was desperate to get Ryan up in court. The bungle of letting Annie Murphy die was bad enough; they didn't need the Shiraz woman getting herself arrested and going on about how the body wasn't even there at the time of death. If her husband hadn't co-operated they'd have done something else to discredit her story – they'd have had to.' He was standing a little too close to me again, the way he had earlier, only this time I was seated and because of the light he seemed to loom over me. 'Can I have a turn now please Miss?'

'You may.'

'Who told you she visited the prison?'

'Her sister Siobhan.'

I heard him suck in air. 'She agreed to see you?'

'I collapsed on her. She did me a good turn.'

'You wouldn't happen to be able to identify where exactly...'

'No, I wouldn't. I thought you were leaving. Surely you don't need to know this?'

'Call it curiosity,' he said, but the lightness sounded forced.

'Next question,' I said.

'Who have you discussed this with besides Victor?'

'No one. It's odd hearing you call him Victor. Everyone I know calls him Vic.'

'What about written evidence?'

'"Evidence"? Do you mean have I stashed notes somewhere? I wish I had but no, it lies ahead of me. . . . Why do you want to know *that*?'

He came even closer and out of the corner of my eye I caught sight of something in his hand. 'Absolutely no one?' he said.

Oh God, I thought as my heart accelerated. I pushed myself to my feet, my eye on that hand. 'What?' I said.

I began to step backwards towards the door – he was definitely holding something shiny – and as I moved, his arm came around and pushed a hard metal point into the right side of my neck. I gave him a shove and attempted to run but as I was co-ordinating my feet, the room began to spin and I felt myself falling down a deep dark hole. Please, please, I prayed, if there's anyone up there, not again. Not this again. Then I passed out.

II

I wake up on my back in total darkness, unable to move, and instantly think, now I really *am* dying – I must be. To allay the fear I concentrate on my body and realise that this time, as before, I'm stretched out in a moving vehicle. The difference is that I don't just have the sensation of being tied hand and foot, I *am* tied hand and foot. Also, my memory's all there.

What a fool!

I bring my criss-crossed wrists to my eyes and squint as hard as I can at my watch. Nine something. I've been out over two hours.

Why are we riding over such bumpy ground? Why am I alive?

The bumpy ride goes on for ever before my abductor finally brakes and cuts the engine. The car door opens and closes, footsteps crunch crunch crunch on the ground towards me, the back doors swing open.

I play dead, hoping to disarm him the way he disarmed me, and

I manage to hold out even when he puts his hand on my right calf and gives me a rough shake. Eventually he curses and stops. The doors bang shut and he crunches back to the cab, again opens his door, crunches back. This time after he swings the back doors open he climbs into the back of the van and shuffles towards me on his knees. I am trying not to flinch from the tobacco smell on his breath when suddenly a wave of cold water lands slap on my head.

I scream and try to sit up but just wrench myself badly.

'Jolly good,' he says. 'Welcome to the world of the living.' He laughs at what he's said as he unties my ankles. 'We find it easier to get people to cover this next bit under their own steam – so much less effort.' He holds a handgun, barrel upright, two inches in front of my eyes. 'However, if we have to drag them, we do.' He waves it at me. 'Come on now my little morally superior one.'

I want to be cool, save my strength, but as I slide out I can't help muttering 'bastard' at him. This makes him laugh even harder. I bite my lip and look off and up into the distance. There's no cloud here, just a clear sky full of stars. It's a moonless night but as my eyes adjust I make out fields to the left and around to the rear of us. In front and to the right is rock which rises until its edges blend into the night.

He nudges me in this direction by poking me in the ribs with the barrel end; I use the forced march to shake the rubbery numbness out of my legs. As we approach what seems to be a large wooden door in the rock face, I feel his attention go to it and without even thinking I take a step diagonally left, which puts me even with him, swing my tied wrists up over my head, and attempt to bring them down on the gun. My angle, alas, is all wrong and before I have a chance to run he's on my other side and I stumble over the foot he sticks in my way. I land hard on my cheek, which rips a bit, and I scream again.

He kicks me in the back of the ribs. 'Get up,' he growls.

'I can't,' I say as I roll over. I will myself not to cry, not to give him the satisfaction. I will myself not to panic about the baby.

He kicks me again on the side.

'You'll have to help me up,' I point out between clenched teeth.

He lets out an exaggerated sigh and, bending, pulls me up roughly.

'Walk,' he says, gun in my temple.

'Vic will report me missing. Vic knows who you are.'

'Correction. Vic knows the traitorous bastard you think I am.'

At first I don't understand. Then I do and the anger and frustration make me wriggle my wrists, as if passion might set me free. What I discover is that the mud from the fall has made the ties (not that firmly in place to begin with) more slippery. There's a long way to go, but if I try . . .

He pushes me towards the wooden door until we are mere inches from it, then inserts a large key.

'Where are we?' I say.

'You've had your questions,' he says. Then he prises open the door just enough for a body to slip through sideways. The smell that rushes out is of earth's bowels: heavy, warm, damp.

Fecund.

He pushes me in, locks the door again behind us and instructs me to stay where I am. As I can't see, I'm inclined to do what he says. Besides, I'm happy for the opportunity to work on the rope. This could be some mad fantasy, but it really does seem to be loosening. He walks away using his little torch and after some time the fuzzy yellow-orange light of first one oil lamp, then another, then another, begin to come on, casting a shadowy illumination across a glistening wet corridor.

By the time he comes back for me, I can separate my wrists about an inch.

He prods me to move and though I obey I take it slow. This is not just because I need time for my wrists but because the ground, which at first I can't quite see, is squishy underfoot. The air is just as sodden – like a rainforest, only without the heat – and elongated droplets of water fall reluctantly from overhead. He has to walk hunched at first but gradually the ceiling of rock above us widens and heightens. Watching it grow more vaulted, I forget about my feet just at the point where the surface beneath them changes from earth-spongy to rock-slippery. First one then the other loses its hold and as I slip I put out my hands. This is just the adrenalin-powered extra jolt that's needed; my hands are suddenly free again and they land on a surface that's slimy like seaweed on wet boulder and I gasp even as I hold myself steady.

In the process of this manoeuvre I've turned my back to my captor and now see that here's my second chance. I hear him approach; I count under my breath; I slide my right hand into my coat pocket. I grasp my keys, finding the mortice with my fingers, then I extract them slowly and as I feel him at my back I turn and jab wildly at what I hope is crotch level.

He grunts 'Jesus!' and the next moment is curled up on the ground. I look for his gun but don't see it. I do see the little torch and snatch it up.

I'm completely disoriented but don't care. I move forwards and to the right, as far as I can, trusting that going in this direction will lead me out of the caves. After two or three minutes, however, I begin to despair. All stalagmites look the same and yet these do not look familiar. The next moment I am facing a dark cul-de-sac.

Oh God, I'm going to have to go back. He doesn't need to follow me. He just needs to wait.

I feel the rock surfaces in the cul-de-sac – this is a really desperate move – but as I am imagining my final moments my hand discovers a crevice. I look in – there is light glowing behind it – there is a hole which with any luck . . .

I ignore the sliminess and the fear of getting stuck for ever and push myself through this hole, head first. There is a bad moment in the middle but eventually all of me is through to the other side.

This is the largest cave so far. Here the lights are already on and in the distance I see what looks from where I am like a catwalk. Behind me I hear footsteps – hear him call – and make for this catwalk quickly.

I pick my way up the wooden steps and put a foot tentatively on to the bridge, which is a plank and two-by-four affair, then hesitate. I hear him again, this time close – *too* close. I turn – his head is through the hole, his torso is emerging. I shuffle one step, then two, then a third. The bridge moves and I reach for the railing. My heartbeat is wild and while I'm trying to bring it under control I look down and realise how long a way down is. At its bottom is a chill blue surface: water – distant water.

I feel the familiar sensation: the desire not so much to jump as to stop resisting jumping. The water seems to be rising to meet me; I can feel it pulling – hear it calling.

I think, if I take a deep breath, let go and run, I might make it.

He's on his feet now. He's coming towards me, striding towards me.

Move legs, move.

I blink hard against the vertigo and take a step, then take another. I'm working on the third when suddenly there's a noise – a bang – though it may be that I see him hear it rather than hear it myself. A moment later I feel a hard, sharp, all too familiar pain on the side of my stomach where he kicked me. I grip the rope railing so tight with both hands that my fingernails dig into my palms just with the effort of trying to stay upright. Then, as I hear him come up the steps, a male voice from the other side of the bridge shouts, 'Halt. Put up your hands, Friedmann.'

I feel myself crumple, as if in slow motion, into unconsciousness, and as I sink there is a second shot, then an exchange of voices, shouting male voices, then another exchange of bangs.

The pain intensifies.

David, I think (for no reason at all). David.

Then I give in to the darkness.

III

This time when I open my eyes I see a young woman in a funny bonnet staring down at me. At the sight of me blinking against the dim light the frown lifts from her brow.

'Ah good,' she says.

I think, the baby.

She says, 'Your two friends have been waiting for you to come to. Would you like to see them?'

Suze and Theresa? (*What about the baby?*)

I nod.

Vic comes in with another man. He's Vic's age but taller and thinner. He needs a haircut, has a two-day-old beard, and looks as if he'd rather be wearing a track suit than the jacket and tie he's got on. 'This is John,' Vic says, 'The real John.'

I open my mouth but all that comes out is a sound like a hoarse duck quacking.

John nods and smiles (lips only), then pulls the curtain around my bed. Our privacy secured, he pulls up a chair, sits down, and leans towards my ear. He smells of breath mints and doesn't match my image of your intelligence services mole any more than his imposter did.

'When Vic told me your suspicions,' he says, 'quite frankly I thought they sounded far-fetched. The internal story was that Annie Murphy had been released in exchange for her father's testimony and been killed a day or two later by her lesbian lover for quite unrelated reasons. The department got the D-notice put on so Ryan wouldn't find out his daughter was dead before the trials of the people he was to testify against. It was accepted that there'd been a cock-up but supposedly it lay in the fact that they'd let her go free without adequate protection.

'To check your theory I came up with the idea of letting the head of the operation, our man Friedmann there, know what you suspected. I established that he had a bug in your flat and managed to doctor a transcript to make it plain you were meeting the departmental mole in Trafalgar Square – he didn't know who it was, I hasten to add. No one knew until yesterday. I then observed the response.'

He leans closer to me. 'You must believe me – it never crossed my mind for a moment that you'd be in danger. My sole aim was to use myself as bait to lure Friedmann to Trafalgar Square where I planned to confront him within proximity of Vic and his tape recorder. You weren't really necessary, just part of the ploy –'

'Gosh thanks.'

He has the decency to hang his head. 'I hadn't appreciated what a chronicle of disasters the operation had been – the accident, the Shiraz woman walking in, the neighbour hearing the shouting – and then you get involved in the case and the first thing you do is the thing he least expects: you get an independent autopsy. He just wasn't prepared for his bodged-up cover-up to be picked apart.'

'Which is why he regarded you as such a threat,' Vic adds.

John sighs. '. . . and I, stupidly, was unaware of the fact.'

Vic says, 'When you didn't show up and he didn't either, we went round to your place. That's when we realised what must have happened.'

'Or *faced* it,' John puts in. 'I think I realised when we were standing in Trafalgar Square watching the hands of that clock on the spire of St Martin-in-the-Fields.'

Vic nods: he accepts the amendment.

'Fortunately,' John goes on, 'I'd been looking into the disappearances story for Vic and the more I'd got into it the more I'd realised that the old departmental in-joke about the bottomless pit in the countryside reserved for cock-ups and embarrassments contained the proverbial core of truth. I'd narrowed it down to three possibilities and arranged for each of them to be watched in turn on various pretexts over a period of time. It was a rough survey, you'll appreciate, but the spot with the most suspicious movement around it was Brockley Hole Caves.'

'*Brockley Hole?* Is that where I was? But surely that's for tourists . . .'

He nods. 'The main caves are open to the public, though this time of year they close in the late afternoon. But the site is vast – there are twenty-odd other caves that only explorers and divers ever see. And it has an ideal feature for the purpose of getting rid of people: a river so deep in parts that divers have never found the bottom. They don't even know how far down the bottom is.'

I remember the pull of that distant ice-blue water. How many would I have joined in there?

'We didn't know about the back entrance he brought you in through. Something like that had to exist but given the pressure of time I concentrated on getting us access through the front door.'

The memory of the shooting comes back to me. 'This man Friedmann,' I say, 'did you kill him?'

'He winged him,' Vic says. 'He's in custody.'

'Whose?'

'Police,' John says. 'Attempted murder.'

I smile at that.

'It's all right for some,' he smiles back. 'I've been suspended "pending an investigation into a series of departmental leaks".'

I make a sympathetic noise, but can't help myself – all I can think of is the legal fight ahead. I can't see it actually making it to court – I can't see it getting reported either, come to that – but I shall savour it regardless. In fact I am beginning to savour it already when I realise that Vic is bending over me, his frown deep and perturbed.

Even as I say, 'What is it, Vic? What's wrong?' I know. Deep down I know.

He says, 'Why didn't you tell me you were pregnant, Dee? I'd never have invited you to Trafalgar Square, never mind . . .' But he cannot finish.

The truth is now bald: the baby has not been saved. The future I was just getting used to dreaming will not come to pass.

I feel the water welling up from behind my eyes; feel it begin to sting and burn. I blink it away. 'I think you'd better go,' I say.

'Look,' John starts, 'I don't know how to say this . . .'

At the same time Vic says, 'Dee, I'm really . . .'

But I can take no more. I drop my chin to my chest, cover my face with my left hand. With my right I point to the door.